Eat My
Martian Dust

Eat My Martian Dust

Finding God among Aliens, Droids,
and Mega Moons

Edited by
Michael Carroll
and Robert Elmer

BakerBooks
Grand Rapids, Michigan

© 2005 by Michael Carroll and Robert Elmer

Published by Baker Books
a division of Baker Publishing Group
P.O. Box 6287, Grand Rapids, MI 49516-6287
www.bakerbooks.com

Printed in the United States of America

Library of Congress Cataloging-in-Publication Data is on file at the Library of Congress, Washington, DC.

ISBN 0-8010-4528-2

Scripture is taken from the HOLY BIBLE, NEW INTERNATIONAL VERSION®. NIV®. Copyright © 1973, 1978, 1984 by International Bible Society. Used by permission of Zondervan. All rights reserved.

Published in association with the literary agency of Alive Communications, Inc., 7680 Goddard Street, Suite 200, Colorado Springs, Colorado 80920.

Contents

In the Beginning

When I was a kid, I read a book by master storyteller Ray Bradbury called *The Illustrated Man*. The book is really a collection of stories tied together by yet another story. I liked that idea so much that it's rattled around in my head ever since.

One tale is called "The Man," about a spaceship from Earth landing on another planet with people like you and me. The captain is disappointed to discover that the big news of his ship's arrival from another world doesn't interest the nearby village. Apparently, shortly before their landing, another man had come into the village—a mysterious man who changed everything . . . just as he had two thousand years before on Earth.

That mysterious man whom Mr. Bradbury wrote of is Jesus Christ.

This news changes each crew member in different ways. Some become angry. Others don't care. Still others drop everything to meet the Man, to learn from him and give him their love.

Bradbury's story is not about space travel or aliens. It has those things in it, sure, but it's really a story about faith and how different people react when they meet Jesus.

A few years after I read the book, I actually met the Man from Mr. Bradbury's story. My life has never been the same. And so in my childhood a seed was planted in my mind by Ray Bradbury, and that seed grew to be the book you now hold in your hands. Like Bradbury's master work, it's a collection of strange and wonderful stories tied together by another strange and wonderful story.

Ironically, Mr. Bradbury offered Bob and me his story for this book. If "The Man" was a little shorter, and if its language was a bit different, we would have gladly included it in our collection. Instead, you'll have to look it up someday in *The Illustrated Man*.

Here we'll let others tell of adventures in the future, where people of faith find a loving God who is the same yesterday, today, and forever.

Thank you, Ray, for the inspiration.

Michael Carroll
Littleton, Colorado

New Frontiers
Go Where Few Readers Have Gone Before

Beyond Earth's horizon lie other worlds, a wild universe just waiting to be discovered. One day people may build homes and schools, shopping malls and businesses, towns and cities on distant planets and moons. They may challenge the frosty wastes of the Martian polar caps, scale the volcanic cliffs of Jupiter's moon Io, and sail the hidden oceans of Europa. Someday they may even voyage to planets orbiting other stars.

What would we find out there?

What would be important to us? A sense of brotherhood?

Would self-sacrifice, forgiveness, and eternal life matter?

Would settlers of other planets pray to the same God?

This book gathers stories from some of today's finest writers about space and our Christian faith to explore these questions. These are important questions whose answers touch on infinitely more important issues, for wherever humans go, our struggles of faith follow. No matter how far we travel, whether to the pressure-cooker canyons of Venus or the frozen wilderness of Pluto, the promises of

God hold true. After all, the spinning planets and wheeling galaxies are a part of his perfect creation.

The psalmist tells us that "the LORD is the great God. . . . In his hand are the depths of the earth, and the mountain peaks belong to him" (Ps. 95:3–4). Another psalm says, "If I go up to the heavens, you are there; if I make my bed in the depths, you are there. . . . Even there your hand will guide me" (Ps. 139:8–10).

The presence of God on the new frontier will give us hope where there is despair, urge us boldly on when our courage fails us, and guide us through impossibly alien places. And when we are finished with our travel among the stars, we will come to a place where we can rest, knowing that God is even there.

The adventures in this book tell of futures that might be. They tell us of places people might see one day. They speak stories about dreams—and even nightmares—that one day may come true. For now, the stories are fiction. But the science found within these pages is real. Within each adventure, you will find a section called "The Science behind the Story." There you will discover what we know is real today and what might become reality someday. Will you be one of the explorers, inventors, or scientists who helps make that future? Let's go explore beyond the horizon!

Michael Carroll and Robert Elmer
Planet Earth, spring of 2004

We'd been patrolling the outer system for months and months. It gets boring looking for iron-rich meteoroids, surveying asteroids, and all the other things my mom and dad do for a living. My sister, Amy, and I are homeschooled, if you can call this interplanetary crate home.

There was no end in sight to our painful boredom. Then, without warning, what appeared to be a distant asteroid drew close. We could see a regular shape and then antennas sticking out one side. A space station!

A space station apparently abandoned or neglected to get in such a state! It was so covered in dust that the round windows looked like craters on a moonscape; scrap metals had adhered to the sides. This must be a ghost outpost, we decided, and it must have been through a lot.

Dad checked the station's hatches, which still were secure, and found air inside. "We should see what's onboard that can be salvaged," he said, crawling inside. Though Mom protested, Amy and I were already following suit.

The station was dark except for a few faint door lights here and there. Dim orange light bathed the end of a long, dark corridor. Amy tugged my sleeve to pull away from Dad and explore on our own.

"Just be very careful," Dad said in that "I'm in charge" voice.

We were a family of explorers though, and I knew Dad knew we could take care of ourselves. Besides, our radios were on, so we could talk to each other instantly.

Dad ventured through a hatch and left us looking around. The place had an abandoned look, but I felt like we were being watched. Should we have stuck together? That's what always happens in the old movies: everybody splits up, and then they get taken out by some alien, one at a time.

We opened a hatch into a huge, circular room. It must have been the control room. There were a lot of lights blinking, and they all seemed to be red. The monitors were all dead.

"Guys!"

Amy and I both jumped at the sound of Dad's voice behind us.

"Don't do that!" Amy whined.

Dad held up his hands. "Sorry, sorry. I found something you should see."

"Some . . . thing?" I hesitated.

Dad grinned and nodded his head. "It's a sort of doorway into the past, a window into . . . into . . . oh, I don't know. Into adventures and travels. This way."

Dad was a jokester, but I could tell this time was no joke. He led us down a hallway and through a hatch in the floor. Below, there was another circular room. This one had all the lights burning, and by the far wall, in a small chair, sat a small, wrinkled, impossibly old man. His billowing white hair and beard reminded me of a shopping-mall Santa Claus. A grin made its way over the hills and valleys of his face.

"Hello, kids. Welcome to my little world. Have a seat."

We sat.

"This is Mr. Talismort," Dad said. "Mr. Talismort, meet my son, Jason, and my daughter, Amy."

"Pleased. Very pleased. And just call me Talismort, if you will. Haven't had any company for some time, ever since my nav equipment went out. And then there was the fire . . ."

"Talismort had a fire in his communications system, and he hasn't talked to anybody in—"

"Years! Centuries! Millennia! Oh, young ones, the things I've seen in my travels. And I thought I'd never be able to tell anyone about them."

He called us "young ones," but it didn't bother us. After all, he was ancient, and his eyes were the eyes of Solomon, pools of wisdom.

"Things like what?" Amy asked. "Monsters? Aliens? Space bandits?"

"More!" He smiled with his mouth, but his eyes were not smiling. They were looking at something far beyond the room we were in.

Dad said, "I'm going back to the ship for some supplies for Mr.—er—for Talismort. Why don't you all chat?"

"Yes," Talismort said quietly, his eyes darkening, his forehead wrinkling. "Yes, wondrous things. You kids ever been to Mars?"

We nodded.

"Let me show you something from Mars," he said. "Follow me."

We stepped through a darkened doorway and climbed a ladder. Up and up we went through a long tube. In the low artificial gravity of the turning station, it was an easy climb, but we must have climbed the entire length of the craft. As we climbed higher, we passed some very strange contraptions. Springs sprung, gears turned, and liquid bubbled through twisting green tubes. Small lights lined the passageway like long necklaces, sending faint beams of light into the area where Talismort walked. They flickered on and off as he passed.

Talismort waved at the station around him. "I'm a bit of an inventor," he explained cheerfully.

Finally we reached a bright room. Its ceiling was a glass dome, and beyond shone a thousand stars. A shelf ringed the room, and on it were little display cases and pedestals and jars with mysterious things inside. All along the seam where the domed ceiling met the wall stretched a string of the same dim lights we'd seen in the passageway. They brightened as Talismort passed by. It was as if the ship was keeping track of exactly where he was, lighting his way.

"We're in the hub of the station now," he said. "The rest is the chocolate shell—but we've reached the chewy center. Call it Grand Central Station. It's the place where it's happening. Where the rover roves and the cool people hang out."

"That's us!" Amy bellowed. She was obviously enjoying herself.

"Then come have a look. I have lots of things, each with a story of its own."

Our host walked over to a clear case sitting on a shelf, next to many other clear cases.

"It's like a museum," I said.

"No." His eyes sparkled. "An amusement park. A carnival! Each object takes us to another place and time in our minds."

He opened the small glass case, reached in, and took out a reddish stone from a little pile of other reddish stones. His hands were as wrinkled as his face, long and thin like busy spiders, playing over the red stone.

"You see, this is from Mars. Beautiful place, Mars. But there's a problem with all places, and Mars has problems of its own." He held the rock in his hand and squeezed. Sand poured through his fingers.

"Let's sit here under the stars," he said.

Talismort sat in his chair, brushing the brick-red dust from his palms. He put his branching hands behind his head, looked up at the ceiling, and closed his eyes. And new worlds began to open up to us. Distant times, far places, strange planets . . .

"I knew a boy there—back on Mars, that is—by the name of Tyce. Tyce Sanders . . ."

Things Unseen

Sigmund Brouwer

With time running out, Mom wants me, Tyce Sanders, to write these events into a report for a magazine on Earth. She thinks it will mean more to people coming from a guy my age than from any scientist. But I hardly know where to begin. I mean, everything is happening at once. My argument with Mom about church stuff. How it seems my body is getting too weak to move my wheelchair. And how Mom—a scientist herself—has just reported that the oxygen level in the colony is dropping so fast that all of us barely have a month to live.

Let me say this first to anyone on Earth who might read this when we are gone. If you have legs that don't work, Mars is probably a better place to be than Earth. That's only a guess, of course, because I am the only person in the entire history of humankind who has never breathed Earth air or felt Earth gravity.

I'm not kidding.

You see, I'm the only person ever born on Mars. Everyone else here came from Earth about six and a half years ago—twelve Earth years to you—as part of the first expedition to set up a colony. The trip took eight months, and during the voyage my mother and father fell in love with each other. Mom is a scientist. Dad is a space pilot. They were the first couple to be married on Mars. And the last, for now. They loved each other so much that they married by exchanging their vows over radio-phone with a preacher on Earth. When I was born half a Mars year later, it made things so complicated on the colony that it was decided there would be no more marriages and babies until the colony was better established.

Complicated?

Let me put it this way. Because of planetary orbits, space ships can reach Mars only every three years. (Only three ships have arrived since I was born.) And because of what it costs to send a ship from Earth, cargo space is expensive. Very, very expensive. Diapers, baby bottles, cribs, and carriages aren't exactly a priority for interplanetary travel. I did without all that stuff. Just like I did without a modern hospital when I was born. So when my legs came out funny, there was no one to fix them. Which is why I'm in a wheelchair.

It could be worse, of course. On Earth, I'd weigh ninety pounds. Here, I'm only thirty-four pounds. That makes it easier to get around. At least when my body and arms aren't weak from lack of oxygen.

The other good thing is that I never have to travel far. Not like on Earth, where you can go in one direction for thousands of miles. Here all fifty of us—mainly scientists and workers—live under a sealed dome that might cover four of your football fields on Earth. (I know all of this about Earth because of the CD books I scan for hours every day.)

When I'm not being taught by my computer, I spend my time wheeling around the paths beneath the colony dome. I know every scientist and worker by first name. I know every path past every minidome, the small, opaque plastic huts where people live in privacy from the others. I've seen every color of Martian sky through the super-clear plastic of the main dome above us. I've spent hours listening to sandstorms rattle over us. I've . . .

I've got to go. Mom's calling for me to join her for mealtime.

I put away my notebook and wheeled out of my room. Our minidome, like everyone else's, had two office-bedrooms and a common living space. Mom was waiting for me in one of the chairs outside my room.

I grunted as I pushed the wheelchair. It was getting harder and harder to move it. I worried that pretty soon I might not be able to move it at all.

I finally reached her. She handed me a plastic nutrient tube. Red.

"Spaghetti and meatballs?" I asked.

She nodded. (I've never tasted real spaghetti and meatballs, of course, so I have to take Mom's word for it that the nute-tube stuff isn't nearly as good as the real thing.)

As usual, she prayed over it.

As usual, I didn't.

As usual, it made her sad.

"Our oxygen level is dropping faster and faster," she

said. "How can I convince you to consider faith in God? If we only have a month left . . ."

"I believe only what I can see or measure," I said.

In the colony, I was surrounded by scientists. All their experiments were on data that could be measured.

"But faith is the hope in things unseen," she said. "Otherwise, it wouldn't be a matter of faith. We don't see your dad, but we know he loves us, no matter where his cargo ship is. Faith in God is like that."

"Mom . . ."

We had argued about this a lot. Mom knew she could never force me to believe something if I didn't want to. Nobody can make another person believe. They can make another person pretend to believe. But Mom preferred to keep our discussion going by letting me express my doubts. Faith, she said, grew stronger through doubt.

I ripped off the top of my nute tube. Most of the scientists needed to use a knife. I didn't. My arms and hands were much stronger than theirs because I had been in the wheelchair as long as I could remember.

I guzzled the red paste. "I'm going," I said.

Mom and I were good friends, but we were both grumpy from our big argument and the oxygen problem. I needed time by myself.

She didn't ask me where I was going. She didn't need to. There isn't much room in the dome for me to get lost.

By the time I wheeled to the center of the dome fifteen minutes later, I was sweating from the effort. Before, it would have taken only a couple of minutes and hardly any muscle power. This oxygen thing was scary. But what could I do about it?

Around me scientists walked on the paths, going from minidome to minidome for whatever business they usu-

The Science behind the Story

Eat My Martian Dust!

In "Things Unseen," Sigmund Brouwer gives us a taste of some challenges future Mars colonists may face. One very real problem for people and equipment is the Martian dust. Mars is covered by a thin layer of dust as fine as flour. In the spring, Martian winds kick up dust storms that can cover the entire planet for months at a time.

Martian dust is so fine that engineers must design spacecraft to be "dust proof." In 1973 *Mariner 9* settled into orbit around Mars to make the first detailed map of the planet. The photos it sent back showed a raging dust storm covering the canyons, craters, and mountains. You think it gets bad under your bed? Just try Mars. At the time of *Mariner 9*'s first photos, engineers were building spacecraft to land on Mars within the next two years. The two *Viking* landers had to be fixed to survive those storms. Scientists made dust shields to cover the cameras and various instruments. *Viking 1* and *Viking 2* landed in 1976. Sure enough, they became covered with a thin layer of fine powder after just a few weeks on the surface.

Orbiting spacecraft show great fields of sand dunes marching across craters. Many craters and rocks are covered by the dust and sand, and the dark markings on Mars—the ones early astronomers thought were canals—are actually shifting dust of different colors.

The air of Mars is very thin, but its sky is a bright tan color because so many dust bunnies float in the air. Each night the sky turns blue just after sunset. It's pretty weird having a sunset-colored sky during the day and a blue sky at sunset! It's all because of the ever-present dust of the red planet.

ally had. They nodded or said hello as they walked around me.

I nodded and said hello back. Other than that, I just stared upward at the purples and oranges of the clouds above the dome. Other people on other expeditions might one day explore the planet outside. Not us. For starts, we would be dead soon. Dad was piloting the next cargo ship, and it wouldn't arrive for two months. One month after the colony dome ran out of oxygen.

I kept staring upward. My eyes drifted to the giant, dark solar panels that hung just below the clear roof of the dome. These solar panels were killing us. They turned the energy of sunlight into electricity. Part of this electricity powered our computers and other equipment. Most of the electricity, though, went as a current into the water of the oxygen tank. The electrical current broke the water—H_2O—into the gases of hydrogen and oxygen, two parts hydrogen for every one part oxygen. The hydrogen was used as fuel for some of the generators. The oxygen, of course, we breathed.

But something was wrong with the panels. Nobody could figure it out. When taken down and tested, they worked perfectly. But back up at the roof, the panels made less and less electricity each day. With less power, we had less oxygen. It was that simple.

As I stared at the panels, wondering about the problem, I heard huffing and puffing. I turned my shoulders to see bald-headed George, a computer tech, pushing a cart toward me.

He caught my glance. "Either these carts are getting heavier," he said, wiping his brow, "or there's even less oxygen in the dome than we figure."

He pushed on.

Everybody is losing strength, I thought, *not just me.*

I fought a burp as I felt my stomach rumble from the spaghetti and meatball paste.

Hang on, I thought as I remembered lunch. If I was getting weaker, how come I'd been able to rip open my nute tube like always?

I thought about it some more. What if it wasn't me getting weaker but my wheelchair slowly getting harder to push? And what if George wasn't losing oxygen but the cart was harder to push?

Weird, I told myself. Why would things with wheels be getting harder to push? And how could it be happening so gradually that we didn't notice?

I heard a squeak high above me. I looked up. I heard one more squeak. From the solar panels?

I had a wild idea.

"Mom!" I shouted. "Mom!"

As fast as I could, I wheeled back toward our minidome.

Two hours later Mom came back from her laboratory. I was sitting on the bed because my wheelchair was still at the lab.

"Well?" I asked.

"Things unseen," she said, smiling. "Microscopic particles of Martian sand have gotten into the sealed dome over the years. We took apart your wheelchair axle and examined the grease that helps it turn. The sand has worn it down."

"Wheelchair wheels," I said. "Wheels on a cart. And the tiny wheels that let the solar panels follow the sun! The more sand, the harder it is for all the wheels to turn."

"Exactly," she said. "That was the squeak you heard. We

were looking for the problem in the panels, and all along it was something as simple as the grease for the wheels. Technicians have already fixed the problem!"

She high-fived me. I hardly noticed, I was thinking so hard.

"Things unseen," I said. "Isn't that what you just said? Things that are there but you don't know it until you know where or how to look?" I grinned at her, finally understanding. "Like we don't know enough about what's behind faith but someday we'll find out?"

She high-fived me again. It was answer enough.

Talismort's eyes mirrored the stars above us. He was smiling, remembering his friend on Mars, or maybe remembering something else. He seemed to have lots of memories stored under that long, silvery hair of his.

"Where's my pipe?" he mumbled. He patted his pockets, searching. As if awaking from a nap, he looked at us and said, "Come up these stairs, and I'll show you something."

There were so many objects in the room, peculiar rocks and alien-looking utensils. I wanted to stay and explore, but Talismort was already on his way. We followed our host through a very small, round port and up a winding stairway. Around and around we went. The steps were metal grids, so you could see through them, all the way down. The higher we climbed, the more dizzy I got. The turns of the stairway were very tight. Amy's feet were right in front of my face.

"Just up here," Talismort encouraged.

More of the little lights flickered on and off as he passed. They looked like strings of pearls, which is what Amy called them. Pearl lights. I heard a clang up above, and light flooded into the stairwell. I thought we would see another room with pictures or displays, but these stairs led to a library. The room had the normal library screens, but it had something else: shelves and shelves filled with real books!

Even more interesting to me was the food port in the

wall. Talismort punched a few keys and pulled two mugs of hot chocolate from the port.

Talismort sat down at a pseudo-wood desk and pulled a smokeless pipe from a drawer. He put it to his mouth and flipped the toggle on the bowl. An orange glow drifted up as he closed his eyes. "You know, smoking used to be bad for you. People would actually burn leaves in a pipe like this, and smoke would come out."

"I always wondered why they called it 'smoking,'" Amy said. "Our dad used to smoke a pipe, but there was never any smoke coming out. He said it was like chewing gum."

"Good thing." Talismort jabbed his pipe at her. "More healthy that way, with no smoke." He looked into the glowing bowl. Orange light flickered in his deep eyes. His voice became a whisper, like a breeze drifting through a window that someone forgot to shut tight. "There are planets that smoke. Entire worlds that burn with sulfur and brimstone. Places with fire . . . and lava . . . and poisoned fumes." He gazed deeply into the small light, and we knew he was looking not into his pipe but into the past.

"Are you talking about Io?" I asked, trying to show my scientific expertise.

He was quiet for a very long time. "This ship has traveled farther than you can imagine. Io is a mighty violent place, all right. All those volcanoes on that little moon, and so much radiation from Jupiter. Jupiter fills the sky there, you know. But I was thinking of another place much farther afield. It's a planet called Three Zed that orbits another star. And on that volcanic rock of a world is a domed city called Baseline Settlement."

Despite the warm mug in my hand and the hot chocolate in my stomach, I felt a trickle of ice roll down my back . . .

Their New Masters

Kathy Tyers

A black streak blotted out the stars overhead, flying fast and low. Wind Haworth dashed along the crater's rim toward a good hiding place, spotted a jagged boulder barely in time to avoid running into it, and dropped to her hands and knees. She listened hard, holding her breath.

The ground vibrated, but there was no hiss, no horrible whoosh from an air leak. She hadn't torn her vacuum suit.

"Are you still with us?" Echo Willis's voice whispered inside Wind's helmet. Wind spotted Echo crouching close, behind a boulder of her own.

"I'm fine," Wind told the older girl. *Just in too much of a hurry*, she scolded herself. With its volcanic history and toothy geology, Three Zed was an airless world where stupid people died young.

So why am I sticking around? She glanced over her left shoulder. Below lay a two-year-old crater, its lava floor still too hot to walk on, even wearing boots. Two years ago a city stood there.

"Here comes another one!" Scratch Drossin, the oldest, sounded farther away. Wind crouched again.

A second wedge-shaped patrol craft passed over their heads. Landing lights made white streaks on the crafts' silver bellies, and red and yellow flashers traced their wings as they swooped toward Baseline Settlement. *We aren't doing anything illegal!* Wind reminded herself. After the ground stopped shaking, she rose up on her hands and knees.

Three Zed had been conquered. The Elleh, "others" in the old tongue, were hated invaders—offworlders—but supposedly related to her own people.

All I would have to do, she reminded herself, *is promise to obey them—and their god. The biggest bully always wins.* She eyed the crater's scorched floor one more time. *That god must be awfully big.*

Religion was for weak people though. Wind longed to be strong.

She peered out at Baseline Settlement's dome glimmering near a distant mountain's foot. Between Wind's home settlement and the hot crater lay a plain scattered with wreckage and debris blown out in the Golden City's destruction. The debris made for good bargaining with the Elleh. Prospecting was a youngster's job, and Wind was the youngest person left on this dying world, except for one sick little nephew. Two years ago, the Elleh took all the young children offworld to protect and "educate." They claimed Three Zed had no true families to separate.

Wind resented that. She had a clan, even if she couldn't

point to her genetic mother and father. She had friends like Echo and Scratch.

Not that she trusted them. On this world, the strongest had all the rights.

Flying fast and low, the patrolling pair circled Baseline Settlement twice.

"They're attacking again," Scratch muttered. "I knew it."

The thought made Wind's stomach hurt. "They aren't shooting," she pointed out.

Echo stood up and slung a bounty bag over one shoulder. "Let's head back."

Wind groped under a rock for her own bag and followed Echo down off the crater's rim. Scratch vaulted into his six-wheeled crawler and started it as the others climbed aboard. Instead of heading out across the black plain, Scratch steered into a boulder field that angled toward Baseline Settlement.

"They won't spot us down here," he mumbled as they bumped along.

Wind hunched in the backseat. The distant sun gave little light, so even tall rocks didn't throw enough shadow to really hide a crawler. Far off to her right, Baseline Settlement's dome skin scattered inside lights to glow like a large, flattened lamp. She watched for flashes that might mean a battle inside. Seeing none, she flipped her hand, idly sending a burst of thought into the door panel's circuits. A dim green light glowed.

Big deal. Turning on a light by brainpower was the easiest of the ancient ones' Talents, now forbidden by Elleh patrols. Wind's former masters, who had lived in that vanished city, had named her clan Haworth—Half Worth. She was lucky to be alive at all. *At least it's safer to be a kid here than it used to be.*

She switched her headset to Haworth frequency.

Through hissing static, she heard the last half of a sentence. ". . . will be changed if there are new developments." Long pause.

She switched back to her local interlink. "Listen." She interrupted Echo and Scratch's argument. "Something's going on, all right." She heard two clicks as her friends linked to Haworth's frequency. Static hissed for a few more seconds, and then the message repeated. "Air contamination incident. Keep indoor masks at hand until further notice. All personnel now outdome, stay outside the main airlocks until further notice. This statement will be changed if there are new developments."

"That's not good." Echo's voice sounded low and glum.

"Look." Scratch pointed ahead.

Wind could see the landing pad near the dome's Inport. Standing guard beside the two wedge-shaped patrol crafts, half a dozen Elleh were easy to spot in their midnight-blue vacuum suits. Some carried weapons.

"That," Echo said, "doesn't look like a domestic air problem."

"I hate being stuck outside," Scratch muttered.

Wind straightened. "There's another way in."

The older kids' heads turned.

"There's a tunnel to Main Air. We're supposed to use it for maintenance if everyone inside is ever put down by bad air and we're caught outside."

"Why don't I know about this?" Scratch demanded.

"It's Haworth business." Wind's clan might be half-worthy servants to the Golden City's rejects, but they did maintain Main Air.

"Right," Scratch said. "All right, then. You lead."

With their crawler parked deep in the rocks and their bounty bags forgotten under its seats, the three of them crept into the tunnel. Wind led the way, feeling along its stone walls. Echo's hand rested on her shoulder.

"I told you it was an attack," Scratch grumbled from farther back. "Listen, they took everybody who would make that Obedience to their god. They're just going to wipe out the rest of us."

Echo sounded irritated. "If you were them, wouldn't you scatter us? We stole their ships, splashed their civilians—"

"Put a hatch over it," Scratch growled.

Wind stumbled. "Watch out," she whispered. "There's a step."

Echo was right though. Golden City soldiers had taken her cousin Reef for a suicide mission three years ago. They had stolen Elleh ships. They had massacred Elleh men, women, and children. When the strongest ruled, everyone else here or on the Elleh's planet was expendable.

The Elleh claimed to follow an old, old law. *The ancient ones were made by a great god,* they claimed, *for a great purpose. All people fell from it, but we—the Talented—fell the farthest. Our Talents were part of our people's great sin.*

So who was scarier? Relatives who could waste you for no reason or strangers who wanted your very soul? Family who would have left your weak little cousin outside to die or soldiers who kidnapped every toddler they found? The Elleh wanted to take Wind and all her kind far, far away. When they took over Three Zed, she was twelve, just old enough for the Elleh to call her "accountable" and give her the choice.

She still hadn't decided. Really, there was only one person she could count on.

Herself.

Faint lights gleamed around the edges of the tunnel's metal door. Wind faced the code panel and said, "Haworth." The door slid open. Brilliant lights switched on inside a small chamber.

Scratch pushed past Echo and Wind into the airlock. Wind closed it with another word, then cycled it.

"Now what?" Echo murmured against Wind's ear.

Wind kept her voice low too. "From Main Air, we can get to our clan blisters—"

The airlock's inner door opened. A steel tunnel took them through a room full of humming machinery. On the master board, main dome functions looked fine, but Haworth Blister—a smaller dome inside the settlement, where Wind's clan housed—had a massive load of organic dust in the air outside its tech and housing buildings.

That was weird. She frowned. "If Haworth's air fresher overloads, it will automatically vent out into the dome."

"Can't Main Air handle it?" Echo asked.

"Depends," Wind said. "I mean, probably. It was built to handle it."

On Three Zed, every building had its own air safety network. Her clan must be scrambling to fix things inside the housing blister. It seemed strange that the air maintenance clan would have an air problem.

"Come on," Scratch said. "Move."

At Main Air's entry, they scattered. Wind dashed up the settlement's bare pavement to Haworth Blister. She kept her vacuum helmet on. Once inside the blister, she groped toward her housing building. Green murk hung like smoke in the blister's air. This was a disaster! Where was everybody? Her whole clan should be scurrying behind the tech building's big windows, fixing the problem.

She cycled through one more airlock into the housing building and took a quick look around the courtyard. Cloth streamers dangled from its ceiling. Clan trainers used them to point out airflow patterns, but Wind liked to sit on a courtyard bench and watch them dance.

Several dozen people stood around the benches. Some wore outside suits. A woman carried hers like a limp body slung over her shoulder. Everyone wore an indoor-rated air filter around his or her throat like a necklace, ready to pull up over nose and mouth. Day lights from out in the dome, tinged weirdly green, shone through a high window.

Wind pulled off her outdoor helmet and tucked it under one arm.

A tall man marched up and said, "Just the person we wanted to see. Come here." He grabbed her arm and pulled her forward.

"Ouch," she muttered. "Let go."

He grinned, tightened his grip, and kept pulling.

Around the farthest bench stood several more men. One had charcoal black eyes and light brown hair. She frowned. Glyph Bar-Scoria was known at Baseline Settlement as the loudest of the anti-Elleh rebels. Dowda Haworth, the clan matriarch, had warned Wind to avoid him. As the second-youngest Haworth, and not particularly strong or smart, she was easy prey for troublemakers. The Dowda stood not too close to Bar-Scoria now, crossing her arms and scowling but plainly not trying to shut him down.

Then she was afraid of him too. *Here we are, following the strongest,* Wind thought, feeling small indeed.

Wind's irritating escort released her arm. "Look who turned up," he said.

Bar-Scoria stood up. Nearly two meters tall, he looked bony even inside a baggy black pressure suit. An outdoor-rated breath mask dangled from his hand. "Glad you could join us," he said. "You probably noticed we're under attack."

Wind wished Scratch and Echo were there. "We saw two patrol ships come in, but—"

"They did something terrible to Haworth Blister's air fresher," Bar-Scoria said. "The membrane's dying. Good thing you were outside."

"Huh?" she asked. Inside each clan blister's tech building, the air fresher held a living membrane. It digested waste gases and other unbreathable stuff, then vented it into the Baseline dome.

"It's a good thing there was a Haworth outside," he repeated. "Somebody who knew how to get in, even when they locked us down."

"I don't understand," she said. And where was everybody? She recognized only Dowda Haworth. She wished she'd inherited stronger Talents. People like Scratch could easily read someone else's emotions.

Bar-Scoria crossed his arms over his black suit. "Those unspeakable Elleh dumped plant debris from the food-synth plant into Haworth Blister's big fans."

If Haworth's air unit failed, that could clog the main one in no time.

As Bar-Scoria's goons closed in around her, Wind was too scared to do anything but nod silently. She knew one thing: the Elleh had no reason to foul the air in here. Bar-Scoria had to be lying.

Why?

"The Elleh keep saying they're going to protect us . . . from each other, from problems like this," he said. "It's time for them to show us they mean it. We sent a distress call over to Inport, but they haven't answered yet."

So maybe the fearsome attackers were just tech help, called down from the Elleh's big ship up in orbit.

Wind shook her head. "I'm pretty far along in my training," she said. "I'm small enough to crawl into air ducts and strong enough to shut down the flow out to Main Air long enough to get someone in here and fix things."

"We can't fix the membrane," one of Bar-Scoria's men answered. "It's half dead. They're going to have to clone a new one."

A smaller man stepped out of Bar-Scoria's shadow. "They invaded us. Stole our heritage. Everything that sets us apart from ordinary people, like our right to do this," he said, dropping his air mask toward the ground but catching it in midair without touching it. As he held one hand open, the mask levitated back into his grip. "Or to read the shebiyl. Those are the strengths that matter."

Wind shivered. Reading the shebiyl, fuzzy glances of future events, was a rare gift that the Elleh called evil sorcery. They claimed that Wind and her people were slaves to evil and that every person old enough to choose had to reject evil for himself or herself. If the Elleh knew Bar-Scoria had a shebiyl reader there, they'd all be locked up.

"The shebiyl," Bar-Scoria said softly, "says this is the time to get rid of them, before they wipe out the rest of us. Are you with us? Or," he added, as another of his men gripped her shoulder, "are you against us?"

Trembling inside, she managed to say, "I still don't understand what you want me to do."

Bar-Scoria threw his breath mask to the floor. "You are so stupid," he exclaimed. "In the old days, you'd be dead by now. We used to take stupid people and use them for experiments. Remember?"

She gulped and nodded. In the old days, not even Dowda Haworth could protect the clan brood from Golden City scientists who came looking for "volunteers."

"I need someone," Bar-Scoria said, "to hand carry another distress call over to the Elleh at Inport. Somebody convincing. Obviously, you know how to look scared."

Somebody chuckled. Wind raised her head and frowned, crossing her arms.

"You're also little enough," Bar-Scoria said, "to get sympathy. Especially if you go crying to that mush-hearted admiral about all the Haworth techs trapped inside Haworth Air."

Was that why she hadn't seen any of her relatives? Was he holding them hostage?

Yes, she realized. He was doing just that. In his eyes, inferiors were worthless.

One of his men stepped forward, holding a child to his shoulder. It had to be her little nephew. When Tember was born, the clan swore to keep his existence secret. It helped to know the invaders hadn't taken all their children away.

Tember squirmed, wheezing out a cough.

Wind frowned again. Tember had twitchy lungs. If the blister's air went bad, Tember would suffer. "You should take him to another blister," she suggested.

Bar-Scoria scowled, and embers seemed to glow in his charcoal black eyes. "He'd have to cross the stink zone inside this one to get out. And all the infant-size breath masks somehow disappeared."

Where did you hide them? she wanted to shout. *You're the biggest bully left on Three Zed!*

"What do you want me to do?" she growled.

"We want our world back," Bar-Scoria said. "Don't you?"

The Science behind the Story

Funky Filters for Fumes

In "Their New Masters," Kathy Tyers envisions a domed city where fresh air comes from biofilters. When things go wrong, people have to breathe through masks. In space or on worlds that have an atmosphere that we can't breathe, this is reality!

The International Space Station has designs that can help a crew survive an air contamination incident. The air is constantly moved around by fans, and all air passes through fancy filters called high efficiency particle air (HEPA) filters. There are lots of hidden enemies in the air. Astronauts—or colonists in a dome city—run into nasty germs, or microbes. Microbes can cause sickness, and in a closed place they can get out of hand, growing in all kinds of nooks and crannies. Microbes ride around on particles of dust. Astronauts might inhale the germs or drink them in their water, so the station's filters pull them out of the air and water. In space, where there is a limited supply of fresh air, astronauts must rely on filters to keep it clean.

What about future filters? In "Their New Masters," the air in Haworth Blister stays fresh through a biological air filter. Author Kathy Tyers is describing something that has already been invented: a plant! The leaves on plants and trees breathe in carbon dioxide and breathe out oxygen for us to breathe. They also filter out tons of pollution and dirt from the air. In the future, it's possible that space habitats will grow special membranes based on plants as a perfect filter. Hey, it works for Earth!

"Of course." The Elleh were easy to hate.

But so was Bar-Scoria. When little Tember sneezed and snorted, the man handed him off to Dowda Haworth. The clan matriarch gave Bar-Scoria a withering look, pulled a cloth from her deep pocket, and wiped the little one's messy nose. Finally Wind sensed a flicker of someone else's emotion: Dowda Haworth's anger replaced Wind's own fear for an instant. It gave her courage.

It's a trap, she told herself. *Bar-Scoria wants to lure an Elleh crew into Haworth Blister and fight them where they'll wreck Haworth property*. The idea made her stomach churn.

But somebody had to save Tember. "All right," she said. "I'll carry your message." She didn't tell him about the other ideas flashing through her mind, and she tried hard to shut them off. If Bar-Scoria or one of his goons could read the shebiyl, he probably was reading her fury right now. Not even the Elleh's laws could stop strong Talents from sensing others' emotions. It just happened.

"That's the spirit." Bar-Scoria stretched out a hand. One of his men tossed him a fist-size metal cylinder. "Take them this," he said. "There's an urgent request for repairs inside. And just to make sure you look scared . . ." He snatched her helmet, tossed her the breath mask he'd thrown down, then stalked over to Dowda Haworth. He grabbed the struggling toddler and handed him to a man in a breath mask. "In five minutes, Haran here is walking outside. Into the stink. Carrying the baby."

Wind took half a step forward. "You can't do that," she protested. "That'd be—"

"Four minutes," Bar-Scoria said, "and fifty-eight seconds."

She spun around and dashed toward the airlock. As she yanked on Bar-Scoria's breath mask, she heard laughter behind her.

The mask wouldn't seal to her cheeks. As she ran, she tried to hold her breath, but she had to take one gasp before she reached Haworth Blister's main airlock. The air tasted like she'd hurled into her helmet. Gagging and fighting blind panic, she dove through the lock. Tember wouldn't survive that! She had to save him, whatever it cost. She made it out onto the settlement's pavement and kept running, up the main road toward Inport Blister. Aging machines sat along the road, some of them fallen over. As long as she could remember, Baseline Settlement had been just a slum of the Golden City.

She wished she had her helmet. She could interlink over to Inport.

He's a bully, she repeated over and over as she ran. *He's just a big bully.*

Bullies always ruled Three Zed. They probably ruled everywhere. The Elleh admiral they sent here as governor, a man with a low-Talent reputation, was probably the biggest bully of them all. She was sick of bowing to bullies! What kind of tyrant was the Elleh's god, to blast the Golden City and leave Wind's people to struggle on?

Her feet hurt when she reached Inport. Tiny spots on her back felt hot, as if she could feel Bar-Scoria watching.

Two soldiers, guarding the blister's entry, turned to watch as she dashed closer. They had to be listening with all their senses. These were highly trained Talents, even if they did swear—supposedly—never to use those abilities down here.

I'm not evil, Wind thought hard at the darker-haired soldier—a woman. The other soldier raised one of the dreaded inhalers. Elleh patrols used Talent-blocking drugs on anyone who got close. After all, her people hadn't sworn not to use Talents. She could be a spy. Or carrying a bomb—

She thrust out the metal cylinder. "Here," she gasped. "It's supposed to be a message. And don't waste your blocking drugs. I'm just a Haworth."

The woman soldier waved off the man with the inhaler. "If she's carrying anything dangerous, it's by accident. What can we do for you, miss?"

She hated talking to these people! "Please," she panted. "Send a crew to Haworth Blister. Inside the tech building. It's—"

"Whoa," the man said. Another soldier appeared through the airlock. The guard handed him the message roll, and he slipped back inside. "Slow down."

"I can't," Wind exclaimed. "They gave me five minutes to get you over there—about four and a half minutes ago. Please," she added, and a sob choked her. Poor Tember!

The man raised a pocket link and turned away.

"Forgive me," the woman said, "but I'd better search you."

"Sure. But they couldn't have planted any other bomb on me or anything. Except . . . this!" she exclaimed, jerking off Bar-Scoria's useless mask.

The woman dropped it into a cylindrical container and sealed its lid. Then, to Wind's astonishment, she pulled off her own breath mask and offered it. "Here. Just in case."

Wind eyed it cautiously. Was the filter poisoned?

The woman raised it to her own face and breathed deeply, then lowered it. "It's safe. Really."

Stunned, Wind took it. No one ever did that on Three Zed. She raised her arms and stood with her feet apart. While the woman patted her down, visions of Tember flooded her mind. Tember choking on murky air, gasping out green slime. "Send soldiers too," she blurted.

The woman straightened, raising one eyebrow.

Wind plunged on. "It's a trap. Glyph Bar-Scoria. He's holding most of my clan hostage. We've got a . . . baby in there. They threatened to carry him out where the air's bad. They probably already did. Please, please don't take him away. We're the lowest of the low in Haworth. Having him to play with . . . it just kept our spirits up. Please don't take him . . ."

The woman finished searching her and stepped away. "You can't think we didn't expect a trap."

Wind wiped tears off her cheeks. Was the woman using Talents to calm her down? Back in the old days, she could tell when someone was Commanding. This didn't feel like it, but something inside her was relaxing. They weren't stupid. But they weren't locking her up either. Not yet.

"Come on inside." The woman turned to the airlock. Wind followed, wondering, *Did I just go weak?*

No, she decided. *Somebody had to save Tember. If the Elleh sent unarmed techs, there just would have been more people splashed. Nobody cares about Tember except Dowda Haworth and me. And the dowda can't help him.*

Inport's airlock area looked like Haworth's—a sliding door, a clear-walled waiting area, and a second sliding door. By the time the second door opened, more Elleh had gathered around. Another group hurried up, and Wind spotted a figure she'd seen in broadcasts. Admiral Kinsman had thick white hair and wore a tidy, midnight-blue tunic with a gold star on one shoulder. His eyes were wide under arched eyebrows, and he tilted his head. It might have been an act, but he didn't look like a military bully.

"Thank you for carrying that message, young woman," he said. "We've been praying someone would give us a good reason to go into Haworth Air in force and repair things before they get worse."

She crossed her arms, frowning. *Oh, sure.*

"You know how to repair the problem?" the admiral asked.

She nodded reluctantly.

"And they sent you to us instead of letting you fix it?"

She nodded again. *It's a trap.* She almost repeated it out loud.

"We'll save your little one," he said. "I promise."

Not unless I help, she realized. *It'll take them too long otherwise.* So she told him everything that might matter: where to find Haworth Air's outflow hatch, how many hostages there might be, and where they were probably locked up. As soldier after soldier poured out of Inport's tech building, Wind gaped. So many!

They've been lying low. The voice in her head sounded like Scratch. *They're just waiting to splash us.*

Either that or they only get tough to protect the weak.

Where did that thought come from? she wondered. *They could take you away,* she reminded herself. *Out of here, to safety—*

Oh, sure. Maybe they just took all our children and . . .

And what?

The soldiers massed along Inport Blister's north side, and to Wind's shock, they sliced right through the blister skin at several places. Here and there the ceiling sagged. Tall vertical supports held it up. "We'll fix it," the woman said. "Don't worry. Want something to eat?"

Feeling limp and weary, Wind plodded behind the woman into a housing building exactly like her own. At a dining room halfway up the hall, Wind sat down and tried not to think about what had to be happening across the way, focusing instead on the soup and bread they served her.

"I'm Lieutenant Lucina Claggett." Wind's escort had blue eyes and a surprisingly young face. "You can call me Lucina."

"I'm Wind Haworth."

"That's a pretty name." Lucina smiled.

"You think so?" Wind made a wry face. "Imagine growing up in these domes and blisters." She swept her arms out to both sides. "Not on your big, green, rainy planet. Now imagine naming your baby Air Leak."

"Oh." Lucina pursed her lips. "You must have been just too old to leave with the children. You understand why we took them, don't you?"

"Maybe," she muttered, stirring her soup, hoping BarScoria hadn't killed Tember.

"Wind," Lucina said softly, "we aren't trying to wipe out Three Zed. We didn't blast the Golden City. Your ancestors built it inside a dead volcano. Thousands of years dead. Extinct. It came back to life."

"Huh?" Wind stared out the window at the blister's limp, cut edges. Whether the Elleh's god blasted the Golden City or they used secret weapons like Scratch guessed, Wind now had to deal with people who could revive a dead volcano. Could she trust them?

There was nothing left for her here though. They would steal Tember for sure now that they knew about him.

She clenched one fist on the tabletop. *But I could go with him and protect him.*

No! shouted the inner voice. *What would Echo think?*

"You want us to make an Obedience," she said cautiously. "But I don't want to obey anybody. I want to be strong and free."

"You serve someone with every decision you make."

"The biggest bully left standing."

Lucina pressed her hands together. "Your own selfish nature will become your strongest, cruelest master if you let it guide you." She made her voice soft. "But if you serve the Holy One, he sets you as free as you can be. Otherwise, the things you love best will rule you someday."

Wind stirred her soup and studied the circling vegetables. Even if they took Glyph Bar-Scoria away, the next strongest bully would just step into that power vacuum. *We fed and clothed the Golden City people, took in their weak children, fueled their crawlers, and piloted their ships . . . for what? Pleasing some masters just gave them bigger appetites. Would I do that to myself eventually?*

"We were a powerful people," she insisted.

Lucina spread her hands. "Yes. We were very frightened of you. But none of you was safe except the strongest ones. And they fought each other."

"True," Wind mumbled.

"Wind, each person matters to the Holy One. At the end of your old road, there was only suffering and solitude. We struggle too, but it's on a path we walk together. Our ancient ones—yours and mine, Wind—did things to our genes that were against the Holy One's laws. He promises to walk among us someday if we use our Talents only to serve others. But your people used them to harm others."

Wind shut her eyes. Maybe this idea of serving others was why Lucina gave up her breath mask, why she sat talking with a Haworth instead of locking her up in a cell somewhere.

"All your evacuated people live in a community together," Lucina said. "We're helping them learn to live differently."

And on their world, "Wind" would mean something pleasant. Would she ever stop flinching when she felt air flow?

"How many people who've gone . . . there . . . decided to come back?"

"Not one, so far."

Wind scowled. "You can see why we wonder if they're all just dead."

"Maybe things are so much better there that no one wants to come back."

"Or even send us messages?"

Lucina shrugged. "I'm not sure why the Masters don't allow that. But I'm sure they have good reasons."

One other question bothered her. "What if they make the Obedience but don't . . . go all the way into your religion?"

"They can stay, if they want to."

Two choices: go back to the strongest bully on Three Zed or leave with these people.

They didn't seem as bad as she expected. "What would I have to do?" she mumbled. It probably was something awful.

Lucina's blue eyes got wider. "Really, the first Obedience is simple. You agree to sincerely seek the Holy One's truth, and in the meantime you promise not to harm anyone else."

Wind felt like she'd been hit with a rock. "That's all? That's my ticket offworld?"

Lucina nodded.

"All right," Wind said, bracing herself. "I agree. I promise."

She caught a flicker of the Elleh woman's ecstasy. It made her cheeks flush.

"Tell him," Lucina said. "Tell the Holy One. He's listening."

Wind doubtfully looked all around, decided it didn't matter which wall she faced, then said, "Holy One, I promise to look for the truth and not hurt anyone." Feeling bolder, she added, "So show me whatever you think I can handle." She hesitated. Why not ask for what she really wanted, here and now? "And please, if you're really listening, get Tember out of Haworth Blister alive."

She spent the next hour standing beside a window, watching techs patch Inport's walls. Finally soldiers started streaming back in. Nobody limped. Nobody was carried— no, wait. One soldier carried something in a blanket. Wind sprang up. Lucina followed her outside.

The soldier walked straight to Wind while the rest of her party streamed back into the tech building, smiling and slapping each other's backs. "Here." The soldier handed over the bundle. It squirmed. Tember's nose was streaming, but that was normal.

Wind felt like she'd been handed the power to fly. "Thank you," she exclaimed—to the soldier and whoever else was listening. "Thank you." At the sound of her voice, Tember grinned and grabbed. Little fingernails scratched her chin. "I made us a deal, Ember-Tember. We're going to be okay, I think."

Admiral Kinsman stepped out of the returning group. "Bar-Scoria's headed straight up into orbit—and a jail cell," he said "You prevented a disaster, Wind. And we have excellent medical facilities on Thyrica. Would you be willing to escort your nephew?"

"Yes. I'll be his clan dowda for now." How bizarre—with new masters, she felt strong and safe enough to take charge of Tember.

She whirled around and grabbed Lucina's arm. "Please," she said, "I've got a friend over in Willis Blister. Could I call Echo and ask her to come along?"

"Yes," Lucina said gently. "Of course."

Talismort looked up from the bowl of his pipe. His serious expression was broken by a wink that sent his eyebrow bouncing up and down like a gray ferret. Wrinkles worked their way from his forehead to the corners of his mouth. His mouth, so serious a moment before, pulled into a wide grin. He slapped his knee and laughed.

"Well, back to the hub. I have a few trinkets you might like to see there. Let's take a shortcut. This way."

Walking down another passageway, I could see the pearl lights following Talismort, always tracking him, flashing on the floor and then the ceiling, always lighting his way. Very odd.

Talismort turned into a hatchway that opened into an airlock. "We'll just jump through here into this other hallway."

Like all airlocks, this one had doors at both ends, one that opened in and one that led to the outside. When the inside door was closed and all the air was let out, you could open the outside door and go float around. But this airlock was also like a little hallway. At the far end was yet another door, and that's where Talismort was headed. All along the wall hung a row of space suits, looking like wrinkled, sleeping people. Most were tan, but one was blue, and one was green with a lot of orange dust on it. I wrote my name on the dust covering the helmet's faceplate.

"Interesting suit, that one," Talismort said. "Want to try it on?"

"No thanks," I said. I'd been in enough uncomfortable space suits to know.

He turned back toward the blue suit. His spindly hands played over the folds and creases of the cloth. "Some people think objects can have a sort of memory. I'm not sure I believe that." He was staring at the suit now, his hands cradling the helmet. "But if they did, what memories would these suits have? Perhaps memories of cold, harsh wastelands . . ." He touched the suit like a blind man reading Braille. "Or empty, dry deserts . . ." He moved to the green suit. He gazed into the pitted faceplate. He was looking right through my signature, past the dusted layers of glass.

"This one was a rental. Got it on Mars. Cheap. This pressure suit saw a lot of action, I can tell you. In fact, I will tell you."

············ **3** ············

Zeus's Eagle

Marianne Dyson

In a rented green space suit, Ryan teetered on the edge of Hebes Chasm. The Martian canyon was twice as deep as Earth's Grand Canyon. As he looked down, and down, and down, his stomach tightened.

"Ready?" Sergei asked.

Ryan licked lips as dry as the desert around him. "Sure," he said with false bravado. Seeing a sunset from below the rim had seemed like a good idea yesterday. He'd said yes before he knew he'd have to rappel down a cliff. But Sergei and Amir had insisted there was nothing to it. If he backed out now, he'd look like a chicken.

"Remember," Sergei said in a serious voice, "keep light

off. When Hebe dumps drink, watch for Zeus's eagle to come out of fog."

Ryan nodded. Hebes Chasm was named after the goddess of youth, Hebe. Mythology said she used to be the servant for the king of the gods, Zeus. One day on Mount Olympus, she stumbled and spilled his drink. An angry Zeus dismissed the clumsy goddess. He then disguised himself as an eagle and snatched a handsome Trojan prince to take her place. Martians said that Hebes Chasm was the place she dumped the drink. So at sunset when frosty fog formed in Hebes Chasm, Zeus the eagle came looking for a new slave. Ryan figured the eagle must be some rock formation that was more obvious at sunset. He was curious to see it.

"At least you don't need to worry about being nabbed by the eagle, Sergei," Amir offered. "You're no handsome prince!"

Sergei grabbed Amir by the helmet. "You should talk, you big-nosed immigrant!"

Amir fought to break free.

Ryan envied Amir's easygoing relationship with the Martian-born Sergei. Unlike Amir, who had moved all over two worlds with his diplomatic parents, Ryan had spent his whole life until now in one place. When his parents took research positions on Mars, Ryan hadn't realized how hard it would be to fit in. He was the only Christian at Marineris Middle School. And just because he wouldn't participate in playing pranks on other kids, Sergei called him a chicken. Amir mostly just ignored him. That's why this weekend was so important. Finally he'd have a chance to show them he was someone worth having as a friend.

"Hey, guys, could you leave the beauty contest for later?" Ryan asked. "I don't want to miss the sunset."

"*Da*," Sergei agreed. He released Amir and clapped Ryan on the shoulder. "Good luck, comrade," he said.

Ryan swallowed and whispered, "Thanks."

Sergei placed the cable between Ryan's hands. Then he stepped back, leaving Ryan on the edge in his appropriately green suit.

Sand slipped out from under Ryan's boots as he leaned back. Holding his breath, he pushed off, releasing the latch to feed himself cable.

He lost his grip, and the next thing he knew he was upside down and falling fast—*whap, whap, whap*—against the cliff face. The safety catch jolted him to an abrupt stop, leaving him swinging in midair two miles from the bottom of the canyon. Spots swam before his eyes.

"You okay?" Sergei asked.

Ryan swallowed his fear. "Remind me I make a lousy yo-yo," he said, spinning on the end of the cable.

Amir laughed. "Hebe couldn't manage a clumsier fall!"

Slowly Ryan lowered himself to a ledge beside a big rock slide that fanned out miles below. "I'm down!" he reported.

"Unhook cable," Sergei called.

Ryan did as he was asked. He leaned back in amazement at the mass of rock above him. He'd dropped about two miles. From up there, he must look like a small green pea.

"How's the view?" Amir called.

"Cool," Ryan admitted, now that his stomach had settled. He'd feel better once Sergei joined him.

"Sunrise is even better," Sergei said.

"Sunrise?" Ryan asked. They'd planned to spend the night in a seal-tight cave a couple of miles from the canyon. "Are we coming back in the morning?"

"*Da*," Sergei said, laughing. "To collect your remains! Give my greetings to Zeus."

"Tell Zeus I'm more handsome," Amir added.

The radio clicked off. Ryan was stunned. They'd tricked

him! He looked around at the stark landscape. The ledge was about as far from the rim as it was from the bottom of the canyon. He was stuck here until the other boys decided to send down the cable. It was going to be a long night. He slumped against the cliff face.

Ryan wasn't really in any danger. He'd miss dinner and have to use the diaper in his suit. He'd be uncomfortable but okay. What bothered him most was that Sergei had lied to him. How could he be friends with someone he couldn't trust?

As the sun dropped, shadows painted the Martian canvas with new detail. Ryan spotted a tower of rock that kind of looked like an eagle. If he used his imagination, the shadows made feathers and an outcropping made a beak. He snapped a digital image of Zeus's eagle to send to his grandparents.

The temperature dropped fast in the thin air. Carbon dioxide and a trace of water froze and formed a sort of misty fog that fell to the surface as frost. This was supposed to be the drink Hebe spilled. The daytime pink sky now turned bluish, the opposite of an Earth sunset. Ryan could understand why Sergei had wanted him to come here. There was nothing like this place on Earth.

Soon it was so dark that Ryan couldn't see his glove in front of his helmet. In case the others were watching from above, he didn't turn on his light. He'd never been in a place this dark. There were no distant city lights, no jets flying overhead, no familiar moon. He spotted Earth near the horizon. Ryan imagined the Muslim Amir bowing toward it, offering his evening prayer in the direction of Mecca. Amir's need to face Earth had caused him to become an expert in astronomy. Ryan had learned from Amir that because Mars's orbit was outside Earth's, Earth could be seen only near dusk or dawn.

A weird *ping* sound startled Ryan. What could it be? Mars didn't have any bugs to ram his helmet. It wasn't dust storm season. Suddenly he knew what it must be: Sergei was on the rim kicking sand down on him. For once, Ryan's suit would be the dirtiest. Ryan would be the last one in the airlock and get stuck with cleanup duty. He was sorry if he had made Sergei feel bad by being so neat. He probably expected Ryan to get even. But that wasn't Ryan's way.

While counting the stars, Ryan drifted into sleep.

"Attention! Suit fan overtemp!" a computerized voice shouted in Ryan's helmet. Ryan pressed the flashing button on his chest to turn off the message. His suit fan must have been damaged when he slammed into the cliff. The fan blew fresh oxygen over his face and sucked away the carbon dioxide he exhaled. If it quit, he would suffocate.

He tried the radio. No response. The boys must have gone to the cave for dinner. No doubt they'd check on him later, but later might be too late!

Ryan flicked on his headlamp and stood up. Dust particles swirled around when he moved, like gnats on a dead thing. He paced the ledge, shining his helmet light upward. Even in the low gravity, he doubted he could climb thirteen thousand feet before morning. His fan could stop working at any time though. If it did, he would die in just twenty minutes. The higher he climbed, the better chance he had of his radio signal being picked up and relayed to the others. He decided to climb.

He scrambled over rocks, pulling himself up from one narrow ledge to another. Thankfully, he weighed only a third of his Earth weight on Mars. He swung his legs up onto a ledge but found he couldn't stand up. The cliff bulged out above him. He scooted sideways, shining his headlamp up and down, looking for a way around the overhang. Trying to keep his sense of humor, Ryan called, "Hey, Zeus, the elevator's out of service. How about a lift?" Ryan thought how cool it would be if the real God sent an eagle to pick him up. That might even convince Sergei to believe. But Ryan didn't ask for a miracle. Instead, he prayed for God to show him a path.

Almost immediately he found a sort of chimney carved into the cliff by some ancient erosion. Ryan thanked God for answering his prayer. Then, like climbing a doorway, he braced one foot on each side and walked up. It was slow going in a space suit.

Ryan inched upward for an hour, ankles burning from the strain. He stopped to catch his breath. He carefully put both feet on one wall and his back against the other. He tried the radio. Still no answer. His boot knocked a chunk of rock loose. He followed it with his light as it disappeared into the darkness below. The thin air didn't transmit much sound. He never heard it hit bottom. If he fell, would anyone find him? No, he couldn't think that way. God would watch out for him. He'd be fine as long as he didn't give up.

For the next hour, his world narrowed to small patches of rusty rock caught in the beam of his headlight. His feet throbbed, and his neck hurt from looking up. But he kept going.

"*Wee-oo, wee-oo!*" the suit alarm blared. "Suit fan failure!" The dying fan had finally quit. He had only twenty minutes to make it to the safety of the cave! With the air shut off, his visor quickly steamed up. Sweat stung his eyes. He couldn't see where he was going. "God, can you hear me?" Ryan called. "Please help me get to the cave!"

His foot suddenly pressed against nothing. Ryan tumbled sideways, too exhausted to do anything except fall. Sand and rock and darkness blurred past his visor. Finally he

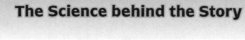

The Science behind the Story

Mountains and Canyons

Hebes Chasma is on the Martian equator, just north of the great Martian canyon, Valles Marineris. It is one of the few places on Mars where the temperature never rises above freezing. The Martian atmosphere is mostly carbon dioxide. It tends to settle in low-lying areas. The Mars Orbiter Laser Altimeter—an orbiting laser that measures altitude—shows that Hebes Chasma is about five miles deep. As the temperature drops at sunset, some of the gas condenses into frost. This condensation would be very dramatic, and it might even produce a momentary fog in a low place such as Hebes Chasma.

Olympus Mons is the tallest mountain on Mars. At a height of over sixteen miles, it is also the tallest mountain in the solar system. It is about two thousand miles northwest of Hebes Chasma. In ancient Greek mythology, Olympus Mons—or Mount Olympus—was the home of the gods. It was where the king of gods, Zeus, lived. Hebes Chasma was named after Hebe, the Greek goddess of youth. Greek myth says Hebe spilled Zeus's drink while serving him on Mount Olympus. Zeus then turned into an eagle and swooped down to nab a Trojan prince to replace her.

The author speculates that people will interpret atmospheric condensation in Hebes Chasma as the goddess spilling the drink, and she hopes there is a rock formation there that someone—maybe you?—will decide looks like Zeus's eagle.

spun to a stop and whacked his forehead inside his helmet. He lay there gasping, dizzy, and afraid to move. Voices came to him as if in a dream.

"Amir, help me with cable," Sergei said. "I heard emergency beacon, and I cannot get answer on radio!"

"I pray to Allah he hasn't fallen off the ledge," Amir said. "Or did you bury him in sand?"

"I am sorry I try to scare him," Sergei said. "Hook me up. I must find him."

"Wait!" Amir said. "There's a light over there. It must be Ryan!"

"He is . . . He is on rim!" Sergei said. "Let us go!"

"How did he get out of the canyon?" Amir asked, panting.

"Suit," Ryan squeaked. He needed to tell them about his suit fan. But he couldn't get his voice to work. "Suit!" he squeaked again.

"Did he say Zeus?" Amir asked.

"Is what I hear," Sergei said.

"Zeus's eagle flew him up here!" Amir said in awe. "How else can you explain it?"

"It is mystery," Sergei said.

Ryan felt someone grab him by the arms and roll him to his side. "His visor is fogged," Sergei noted. "Oh no! His suit fan is off!"

"We must get him to the cave!" Amir said. Ryan felt himself lifted by the arms and legs.

The next thing Ryan remembered was waking up in the cave with Sergei holding an oxygen mask over his face. Then Amir squirted water into his mouth. Ryan moaned. He felt like one giant bruise. Amir gently rubbed ointment on his bloody hands and feet and put ice on his head. Sergei declared the spare suit ready and helped Ryan put it on.

Amir called base and asked for pickup. Unfortunately, their ambulance rover was away on another call. So the boys made a hammock out of climbing cable.

"Okay, Ryan, climb on and we'll trot you back to base," Amir said.

"It's thirteen miles in the dark!" Ryan declared. "I'll be all right until morning." He sat up, and the room spun around.

Sergei sat on his helmet next to Ryan. "You might have concussion. If you were me, would you wait until morning to find out?"

"No," Ryan admitted.

"Well, you say we should treat others way we want to be treated. So we taking you home," Sergei said.

Ryan smiled. Sergei's acceptance of Ryan's way of behaving meant a lot to him. Maybe they could be friends after all. Ryan answered with thanks in Russian, "*Spa-ce-bo*."

"Besides, we can't afford to have Zeus mad at us for messing with his handsome prince!" Amir added with a smile.

"It was God who lifted me to the rim, not Zeus," Ryan insisted.

"Next time I need miracle, I ask you to pray for me," Sergei said.

"I'd be happy to," Ryan said. They were all quiet for an awkward moment.

Then Sergei burst out, "Well, even with boost from God, to climb to rim so fast, Ryan must be Olympic climber. So I hereby dub him Zeus's monkey!" They all laughed.

Ryan thought being called Zeus's monkey was a great improvement over being called a chicken. But next camping trip, he wasn't jumping off any cliffs to earn a better nickname!

The airlock was cramped and dim, and I was glad to make it back to the center of the station.

When we stepped into the hub again, it was dark except for the pearl lights that followed Talismort. He waved his hand in front of a plate, and light flooded the room. Amy was across the room before either of us. She had spotted something.

"Games! Hey, you've got games here."

She was hovering over a chess set. Each piece was a beautiful wooden carving.

"Do you play?" Talismort asked.

"Yep."

"Would you like a quick game?"

I leaned over toward Talismort and said, "Watch out. It may be a very quick game. She's pretty good."

"Pretty good?" Amy squeaked. "I beat you last week!"

Talismort was holding up the black queen. "Such an ancient game, chess. Medieval kings played it. Great generals and common peasants. You can tell what kind of world it came from just by the pieces. The queen and king in their central places, watching over the board." He picked up another piece. "The knight, represented by a horse's head, able to leap and fall upon its unsuspecting prey. The rook, like a little castle, but oh so formidable." He reached to the front line of his pieces. "And then, of course, the humble pawn. It isn't powerful. To some players, it's expendable. But it's a subtle piece. It sits around unnoticed, plods along the board one little space at a time. But if you're not careful, it can put your king in check or even become a queen in the blink of an eye. To me, the pawn is what chess is all about. Quiet strategy. Patience. And then . . . the kill!"

For some reason, Amy didn't want to play anymore.

"Let me tell you about my friends, Randy and John. Randy described a rather creepy game of chess they played."

Chess 4 Life

Randall Ingermanson

It's the Fourth of July, and I'm standing in front of a large tent at the San Diego County Fair, staring at a large, badly lettered sign—"Test your wits against a matched opponent. You could win Chess 4 Life. Only $20."

My buddy John sticks an elbow in my ribs. "Go on, try it, Randy! What have you got to lose?"

For no reason, my palms are sweating. I'm a sophomore at Torrey Pines High School, and I'm the reigning chess champ. This ought to be a cakewalk. But something feels . . . not quite right here.

John pushes me toward the booth and whips out a twenty. "Sign him up!"

A bearded man with greasy hair looks at me suspiciously. "Ya wanna play or don't ya?"

"I'll . . . play." A lead brick settles in my gut.

The man shrugs. "You got a cell phone? You leave it outside, understand? We don't allow no cheating here."

I hand John my cell phone.

The greasy man leads me into the tent. I hear John hollering after me, "Good luck, dude!" I wonder for an instant why he isn't following, but the man is hauling open a big steel door. It's dark inside. All I can see is a gorgeous chessboard. The pieces are some kind of transparent stone, and they seem to be lit from within. As I step closer, I see that the room is divided in half by a large glass wall—kind of like those visitor rooms in prisons. There's a low gap in the glass above the chessboard, just high enough that you can move the pieces. I sit in the large leather chair in front of the board.

The metal door clangs shut behind me. I turn and see that I'm alone.

"Hey!" I jump up and hurry to the door. There's no doorknob. No nothing.

I pound on the door. "Hey! What's going on?"

No answer.

I'm sweating now. What kind of a weird place is this?

"I bet your name is Randy, right?" The voice behind me sounds strangely familiar. I kind of recognize it and kind of don't.

I turn and see a dark shape on the other side of the glass wall. "Who are you? What's going on here?"

He sits down in the chair on his side of the chessboard. "What's going on here is that we play a game. Whoever wins walks out. Whoever loses . . . plays another game."

There's something bizarre about that voice. I've heard it before, but I can't place it.

I stand there staring at him for about thirty seconds.

"Come on, let's play," he says. "You've got two doors

on your side and I've got two on mine. If you win, you get door number one, to the exit. You lose, you get door number two, to another game. What have you got to lose?"

Which is exactly what John asked me five minutes ago, and now I'm in Weird City. I jab a finger at him. "What if I don't want to play?"

He points at the clock. "It's 1:02. At 2:00 sharp, the room fills with poison gas. If the game's not over by then, we're trapped and we die. You've already wasted two minutes. Sit down and let's play."

"How many games have you played?" I ask.

"Just . . . sit."

A sick feeling rises in my gut. I'm gonna kill John for this. I sit down and stare blindly at the pieces. One-hour chess. I can do this. I'm a killer at one-hour chess. This guy has obviously lost at least one game, so how good can he be? I'm playing white, which gives me the advantage. I think for a second and move the queen's pawn forward two squares.

My opponent moves quickly, shoving his queen's pawn up two squares. So he's not stupid.

I move my queen's bishop pawn forward two squares. I know the queen's gambit opener cold. I'm hoping he'll accept.

He moves his king's pawn forward one square, declining my gambit.

Fine. I'm pretty good at this opening too. The very first game I ever memorized was "Alekhine versus Lasker, 1924. Queen's gambit declined." I think for a few seconds and move my king's knight up in front of the bishop pawn.

He instantly mirrors this move with his own king's knight.

I stare at my opponent, trying to get a line on him. The

light's bad, and I can't see much. He's about my height and skinny like me. And he's pretty quick with his moves. Quicker than I am. I wipe my palms on my pants and move up my other knight.

Without hesitation he moves his queen's knight in front of his queen. This guy is fast.

And he's good. We've played out the first eight moves of Alekhine versus Lasker. I'm feeling a little light-headed now. I need time to get a grip. I decide to follow Alekhine's lead a bit longer. I mean, Alekhine was a grand master. This guy I'm playing has lost to some nobody. He won't stand a chance against Alekhine. Eventually, he'll blunder, and then I'll jump on him. I kill his queen's pawn with my bishop's pawn.

The guy takes my pawn back with his, which is the only rational move.

I move my queen's bishop up in front of my knight.

Boom! Quick as anything, he moves his queen's bishop pawn up one square.

We blast through another half dozen moves, with me mounting a kingside attack and him defending. All of a sudden, I feel like vomiting. We're playing Alekhine versus Lasker move for move. And white lost that game. This guy is really good. The kicker comes on move fifteen, when he moves his king's bishop down in line with his queen. A great move but not obvious.

I sit staring at the board for a full fifteen minutes, afraid to move. Should I keep following Alekhine's game plan? Or try to improve on it?

"Dude, you need to move." My opponent is drumming his fingers on the table.

I look at the clock and see that we've got twenty-five minutes left. I decide to stick to Alekhine's game. He can be beaten, but only by a grand master. I move my queen's knight pawn up two squares.

The game unfolds just like I know it. He unleashes a strong attack against my kingside. I move up my queen, poised for my own counterattack. He clogs my attack diagonal with a pawn, and I clog his. I move up my bishop to add weight to my attack. He ignores it, bringing his own rook down to my second row, adding weight to his attack on the knight guarding my king. It's a brilliant move, threatening mate in two. I look at the clock and see I have two minutes left. There's no time to think. I'm going to lose, but . . .

I move my knight to safety. We exchange queens, leaving him with a commanding attack. With thirty seconds left, I tip over my king, resigning.

My opponent leans forward and stretches out his hand. "Nice game, Alekhine."

I shake his hand. In the dim light of the board, I see that he's got a mole at the base of his right thumb. Just like I do.

"Who . . . who are you?" I stutter.

"Listen, there's no time," he gabbles. "So just listen. I'm your future. The loser goes back in time and plays again. You'll get out of this if you just—"

A loud buzz sounds.

"Five second warning!" he screams, running for his exit.

I jump up and spin around. There's a flashing exit sign on my right. I rush for it and hit the push bar at a dead run.

It opens and I'm through. I fling the door shut. An instant later I hear the buzzer change pitch. My heart is jackhammering in my chest. I can't see a thing. There's no doorknob on this side. I turn and stagger blindly, feeling my way along a dark tunnel.

Soon enough, I see another light. An Enter sign. I reach a door. I push through.

I'm back in the room, but this time I'm playing black. The clock says 1:01. And there's a guy on the other side pounding on the metal door, hollering, "What's going on?"

I move toward the chessboard. "I bet your name is Randy, right?"

He turns and looks at me. "Who are you? What's going on here?"

I've figured it out now. I've come through a wormhole or something. I've traveled back in time exactly one hour. I'm about to play my one-hour-earlier self, whose voice I've heard before—he sounds just like I do on a tape recorder. And I'm going to win.

I sit calmly in the chair. "What's going on here is that we play a game. Whoever wins walks out. Whoever loses . . . plays another game."

He just stares at me like a moron. I've been through this already, so I explain the rules, about winning and losing and the poison gas thing.

"How many games have you played?" he asks.

"One. Now sit down and play."

He sits down, thinks for a second, and moves his queen's pawn. I make the countermove, and we're launched. Inside I'm laughing. The poor guy is sweating for nothing. Sure, he'll lose this game and I'll escape. Next game, it'll be his turn. It's weird, but it's totally consistent.

At move fifteen, I push my king's bishop in line with my queen and sit back. My earlier self looks stunned. And I feel for him. I know exactly how he feels. He stares at the board for a long time.

Finally, I say, "Dude, you need to move." I'm getting impatient, drumming my fingers. I'm depending on this guy to lose so I can win. His turn will come, but he just doesn't know it yet.

He looks at the clock, and fear slides across his face. Did I look like that? He puts his hand on his queen's knight pawn and then takes it away. He moves his queen's rook across the back row to stand next to his other rook.

A sheet of raw panic slides through me. He can't do this! That's not what Alekhine played! This isn't the past I just played. In an instant, all my self-confidence is gone. I can't coast through this game. I've got to play. We've got twenty-five minutes left. When that time's up, one of us is going to walk out to freedom, and I want it to be me, because if I lose, I'll be stuck in some endless loop. I'll be playing forever, losing forever, playing . . .

Chess 4 Life.

How can this happen? It's not consistent. This isn't my past, this is . . . some other universe. Some parallel universe.

For a minute, I can't breathe, can't think, can't see. I'm freaking out.

"Dude, you need to move," my earlier self says. Only he's not my earlier self. He's some alternate universe guy. He's drumming his fingers on the table, leaning forward, looking confident. I stare at the board, and my whole brain is frozen. Five minutes tick by. Finally I move my knight up to attack his. It's a stupid move—I should have moved my pawn. We exchange knights, and then he captures my pawn with his bishop. Shortly, he's launched a vicious attack on my kingside.

I don't have the energy to fight this. I stare at the board. Minutes tick by. With thirty seconds to go, I tip over my king. "I resign."

The Science behind the Story

Wormholes, Choices, and Checkmate

"Chess 4 Life" asks more questions than it answers. Could it be? What if . . .? If you watch a science fiction series on TV, sooner or later you see an episode where one of the characters travels through time. The starship hits a wormhole or a cosmic storm, or light-speed travel slows down time.

Sounds good. But before we can understand a wormhole, we have to know what a black hole is. Actually, no one has seen one up close yet, but the theory is that some collapsed stars have squished together so tightly that their surface gravity won't let anything get out—not even light. Thus, *black* holes.

Now, the wormhole idea (it's just an idea) is simply two black holes put together. Traveling through a wormhole would be going in one black hole and out the other. And some scientists with good imaginations guess that time might be different on the other side. Why not? It makes for a few good *Star Trek* episodes.

There are some theories on paper, but no one claims time travel is real science. Even Einstein never suggested how to travel back in time. So time travel is a great "what-if?" that helps us focus on how important even the little things can be. In other words, there are *consequences* to everything, and if we make a different choice, different things could result. That's what time travel stories are usually about. They remind us that what we say and do matters.

The other thing to remember is how our God is outside time. He created it, after all—and the Bible says, "Jesus Christ is the same yesterday and today and forever" (Heb. 13:8). So in that sense, we do know of one genuine time traveler!

"Nice game." He reaches across to shake my hand.

I shake with him, and astonishment flickers across his face when he sees the mole on my thumb. "You're . . . you're . . ."

"I'm your future. You've just made it out, and I'm in limbo."

"You mean like . . . forever?" Horror fills his eyes.

"Looks like it."

He's staring at me like he's killed me.

The clock tells me we've got eight seconds left. "Have a nice life." I stand up.

The buzzer goes off. "Five second warning!" I scream.

Then I'm running for my own exit. I bash through the door and slam it behind me. As I stagger through the tunnel or wormhole or whatever it is, I wonder what went wrong. How many of these parallel universes are there? Two? A hundred? An infinite number?

I'm stuck forever in Chess 4 Life.

I see the Enter sign and punch through.

I feel like I've been slugged. I'm playing black again. The clock says 1:01. My alter ego is pounding on the metal door, hollering, "What's going on?"

I lurch toward the chessboard. "I bet your name is Randy, right?"

He turns and looks at me. "Who are you? What's going on here?"

We go through the same rigmarole, with me explaining and him confused. Only this time, I'm just as confused.

"How many games have you played?" he asks.

I'm too embarrassed to admit that I've already lost two, that I may be doomed to play an infinite number. That I may be playing Chess 4 Life for the rest of my life. Great, I've achieved immortality. "Just . . . sit," I say.

He sits.

We play.

It's Alekhine versus Lasker again, a game I'm thoroughly sick of. I've lost it now from both sides of the board. I'm freaking out.

But so is my alter ego. After I move my king's bishop on move fifteen, he sits staring at the board, realization dawning. Again, I know exactly how he feels, but now that's no consolation. This guy could whip me. I could be here forever.

With twenty-five minutes left, I say, "Dude, you need to move."

He looks at the clock and flinches. He puts his hand on the queen's knight pawn. Moves it forward two squares.

A rush of hope jolts through me. He's following Alekhine. He's chosen to play safe. Chosen to lose.

I move my bishop.

Now the game plays out the way I want it to. I'm watching my opponent, and I see hope dying move by move. He's playing it safe. Forcing me to beat him. And I'm eating his lunch.

With thirty seconds left, he tips over his king.

I'm so relieved I could puke. I lean forward to shake. "Nice game, Alekhine."

He sees my mole and stares at me. "Who . . . who are you?"

"Listen, there's no time," I babble. "So just listen. I'm your future. The loser goes back in time and plays again. You'll get out of this if you just—"

The buzzer cuts me off.

I jump up. "Five second warning!"

Then I'm running to my exit door, I'm slamming through it, I'm bursting out into an empty fairground. There's nothing here. Zilch. I look at my watch. It's 1:00 p.m. on July 6. I can only hope it's the same year. A wormhole can take you anywhere. Something on the ground catches my eye. My cell phone.

I pick it up and see that it's still charged. I flip it open and call home.

"Hello, Ingermanson residence. This is John."

"John, what are you doing at my house?"

A holler pierces my skull.

I yank the phone away from my ear, but I can still hear John roaring, "Randy's calling! It's him! I don't believe it!"

Then my mom is on the line, and she's bawling her head off and blubbering, and it's just embarrassing.

Finally my dad gets on the line, and he's marginally calmer. "Randy, listen. Where are you? What have you been doing for the last two days?"

I swallow the brick that's sitting in my throat and try to sound like I'm in control. "Playing chess," I say. "Chess 4 Life."

I decided to challenge Talismort to a game of chess. We played for about ten minutes. I got the idea he was just being patient with me. In the end, he wiped me out with a couple of clever moves I'd never seen before. It was like playing against our ship's computer.

Talismort laughed, put his hand on my shoulder, and said, "Good game. I've been playing far longer than you have, son, but you show promise."

He walked across the hub. On the far side of the counter stood a glass jar. He waved his hand over it. Light flared inside it, illuminating a stone the size of my fist. The jar began to slowly rotate.

Amy wasn't impressed. "Another rock? No thanks. Geology's not my area of interest."

She can be such a pain.

Talismort gestured toward the specimen in the glass. "Ah, but how about paleontology? The study of ancient life?"

I crossed to the jar. The stone inside was slate gray with a few pockmarks here and there. As it turned in the greenish light, parallel lines came into view. Were they ribs? Marks of waves from some primordial ocean? Spines from a lizard's back? This was more than a stone. It was a fossil.

"What do you think it is?" Talismort asked.

"Looks like the legs of a spider," Amy guessed. But as she spoke, the stone turned farther, and we saw wrinkles. Across the wrinkles were imprinted the pattern of flakes or scales.

"Or maybe," Amy said, "something like a little armadillo."

Talismort looked at me.

I shrugged. "Could be anything."

"Yes, and that's the beauty of it, isn't it? Look again, and you see more. Look yet again, and you must change your mind! It's a trilobite. But no, it must be an insect. Or perhaps an ancient reptilian bird."

The stone offered a new face with faint segments and a bizarre fragmented lobe like a giant bug's eye.

"Yes," Talismort whispered, the petrified thing mirrored in his glassy eyes. "Lobes and fins, scales and bones. It could be anything . . . Sometimes you run across a fossil like that. Sometimes fossils give you bad dreams. Professor Martin Cole had a fossil like that."

Buried Secrets

Shane Johnson

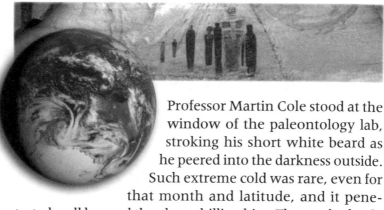

Professor Martin Cole stood at the window of the paleontology lab, stroking his short white beard as he peered into the darkness outside. Such extreme cold was rare, even for that month and latitude, and it penetrated well beyond the glass, chilling him. The sun had only just set, but the brilliant hues it might have painted had been hidden by the lowering gray sky, a gloomy blanket of cloud that had hurried the onset of night.

As the deep, fragile snows disguised the all-but-deserted campus before him, Cole's unwavering gaze was empty, his mind on someone who once had ventured forth from that very room, never to return.

Why?

Golden light splashed against the learned man, cast by flames that danced on the brick-framed grate of the fireplace. The wood there glowed as it flooded the room with sacrificial warmth, its embers angry red, its continual pops and hisses falling upon ears that didn't hear them.

Why did it have to happen?

Cole sipped his customary hot cocoa, his thoughts distant, demanding answers of the silent universe outside.

Why him?

The drink, nearing the bottom of the heavy ceramic mug, grew bitter, and his focus returned to his surroundings. Turning from the cathedral window and toward the large, rectangular worktable in the center of the room, he drew a deep breath, noting how cavernous the room now seemed. How quiet. How lonely. Missing were the sounds of his students, the footfalls, the whispers, the subdued laughter. Early January was such a time throughout the university, and weeks would pass before again the commotion of youth would fill its halls.

The leather soles of his comfortable old shoes made little sound as he crossed the chamber. Like something out of an Edgar Allen Poe story, the dimly lit lab bore deep and innumerable shadows. Bookshelves, filled with texts both ancient and modern, lined one wall, just as they had for the better part of two centuries. Rich layers of varnish covered the wood floor and the wainscoting, lending the dark warmth of days gone by. Draperies of rich maroon, area partitions seldom used, hung here and there from the high ceiling. Storage shelves, added more recently, stood opposite the library, filled with a cluttered yet organized array of tools, supplies, and prized antiquities.

On another wall, a large, framed plaque held a place of honor spotlighted by a lamp. The legend it bore was one Cole had quoted to his class time and again, one he had taught them never to forget in their personal quests for scientific knowledge: "Truth above All."

Taking a moment at the room's large corner sink, he rinsed the now-empty mug, once a birthday gift. A smile forced its way across his lips as again he noted the legend emblazoned boldly on its side: "Professor of the Year." And below that, in smaller print, "What Was My Name Again?"

The gift and the words had come from one Jacob Larson, his former student assistant, whose wit had brightened the lab on more occasions than Cole could count.

I do so miss you, my boy . . .

He returned to the reinforced table at the center of the room, to the considerable object resting atop it. Larger than a man, the block loomed before him, patiently waiting to divulge its secrets.

You were so excited about the find, Jacob. You should be here with me now, solving its mysteries, bringing them to the world . . .

He wrapped himself once more in his work apron and tied the strings with age-knotted fingers. Pausing to activate the video camera that would document his work, he adjusted its tripod and checked the focus, date, and time. The images captured on the tape would prove the authenticity of anything he might discover. Since he had chosen to work alone, with the university shut down and his students away, the watchful lens would be his only witness.

Taking a seat next to the mass of rock, he ran a hand gently along its coarse, ruddy surface. Then, after donning a pair of protective goggles and taking implement in hand, he returned to his task, working gently to remove the hardened casing and expose that which was within.

Such a brilliant young man he was—such a promising future lay before him.

As the whine of the rotary tool filled his ears and the

scent of pulverized dust filled his nostrils, his gaze fell again upon the stone-filled eye sockets that stared into the glare of the swing-arm lamp.

And Cole remembered.

It had been Jacob who first spotted it, there beneath the steady summer sun, almost three years earlier. Cole and six of his students had made the discovery during a fossil hunt in an isolated locale, but it wasn't the bones of some great carnivorous beast that had excited them so. Embedded in Cretaceous stone and barely breaking the surface of the rock, something else had seized their imaginations. Its open jaws seemed to cry out that it did not belong.

A skull.

A very *human* skull.

Brow ridges, cheekbones, nasal cavity, teeth, and collarbone—the visible portions appeared intact, promising a full skeleton. Such a find could push the boundaries of evolution to new extremes. The presence of an ancestor of man in such ancient strata offered an irresistible puzzle, and solving the mystery of how it had gotten there could mean new funding for the university—not to mention a bit of notoriety for Cole himself.

Since no one before them had spotted the remains, they had decided to work quietly—and once they had their answers, only then would they reveal its existence to the world. Such a find, strange as it was, could easily make them all look foolish were it proven a hoax.

In secret, the professor and his students had chipped away, determining the boundaries of the skeleton, freeing the substantial block from the surrounding stone. Then, with pulleys and cables, it had been loaded onto the well-used bed of their truck, fully intact and ready for the long journey back to the lab.

Triumph!

But then, with the impossible prize secured, tragedy had struck.

As Cole and the others tied off the ropes fastening a tarpaulin to the bed of the truck, Jacob mentioned something he'd seen nearby, a glint of something metallic that had caught both the sun and his eye. Off he ran, alone, to see what he could see.

Moments later, a brief shout was all Cole heard.

"Professor! It's amazing—!"

There came a brilliant flash of light and the sharp crack of an explosion. By the time the professor and the others had rounded the outcropping of rock behind which Jacob had been, no sign remained of the student—only a charred, blackened scar bursting wide upon the face of the rock, surrounding a foot-wide hole in the stone.

And that hole opened into a perfectly spherical hollow as smooth as glass, as hot as an oven, and as deep as Cole's reach.

Hoping against hope, he had called out for the boy. No answer came.

I'm sorry, son . . .

Something had been embedded there, something that, apparently, somehow, had detonated—ending a vital life too soon.

I'm so sorry . . .

Cole still mourned.

I should have stopped him. I should have told him to wait for me . . .

He lowered his tools as he closed his eyes, second-guessing every move he had made that terrible day.

I should have done . . . something.

A lengthy investigation into the death had followed. Law enforcement officials had interviewed the professor and his students, examined the site of the dig, checked their records, and reviewed school procedures. No evidence existed that explosives had been in the expedition's possession, and the testimony gathered from the persons involved had harmonized to the smallest detail. How the blast could have been so fierce as to completely consume the young man, no one knew. Exactly *what* had detonated they could only guess, but ultimately, the officials had formed the theory, however insufficient, that Jacob had inadvertently touched off an old cache of blasting equipment left behind, perhaps, a century earlier by miners of the region.

Jacob's uncle, his only family, finally had settled with the university, though no individual fault had been assigned to Cole. The professor too had mourned, wounded as if the student had been his own son. He had taken a prolonged leave of absence, and the skeleton they had excavated had waited in storage, hidden away, under wraps.

Only now, with the distance of time and in the depths of winter's solitude, had the aged lecturer found the heart to pursue the work again.

The whine of the tool resumed. Slowly, as the hours passed, more of the age-darkened skeleton met the air. Throughout the night he worked. And the next night, and the next.

Legs. Feet. Hips. All were revealed to be in amazing condition as the stone fell away.

After a week of careful excavation, Cole found its arms were crossed over its chest. As he labored to free the hands, he came to realize why the ancient figure had assumed such a pose.

It was holding something.

The tool whirred. His picks scraped. Dust rose, and particulate matter parted. His camel hair brush swept away a final residue of tawny powder.

Cole gasped in amazement.

Against the ribcage, secured by both hands, was clutched a disk of gleaming golden metal—perfectly circular, as large as an outspread hand and almost an inch thick.

The professor's heart leapt as his mind ran through a catalog of possible explanations.

Ancient astronauts? Atlantis? Men from Mars?

One by one, he removed several finger bones and the stone surrounding them, finally freeing the object from its prison. After swinging the lamp away, he gently pulled the disc clear and held it up before him.

Words were there upon it, engraved lightly and crudely, as if hurriedly and by hand.

In *English*.

Stunned, he read them again and again: "Twist to Open."

"You've got to be kidding," he whispered. "Now I *know* this is a prank."

Gripping the object in both hands, he played along, did as instructed, and heard a brief hiss as air, long denied, rushed inside.

Vacuum sealed?

Cole's pulse raced. Slowly, with practiced caution, he pulled the front and back halves of the disk apart. The canister was lined with a soft blue substance with which he was not familiar. Nestled snugly at its center was another, smaller disk that appeared to be a single solid piece about a quarter of an inch thick. It too was polished gold in color with an odd, pearly sheen that caught the light. To either side on its upper surface were two small, oval depressions, and between them further words had been etched, also apparently by hand: "Put Thumbs Here."

He set the canister on the table.

This has to be a joke . . .

He glanced at the phone mounted on the wall near the door. Faces flashed in his mind as he wondered if he should call anyone.

"No," he whispered, fearing embarrassment.

Cole reached into a drawer and withdrew a pair of surgical gloves. As he slipped them on, he glanced around the room and through the windows, half expecting a prankster to be watching. Then, after flexing his sheathed fingers a few times, he gingerly lifted the inner disk from its place.

Here goes . . .

He put his thumbs into the shallow ovals.

Nothing happened.

"Now what?" he wondered.

He waited. Still nothing.

Maybe it requires direct skin contact . . .

"If this *is* a hoax," he muttered, setting the mysterious object aside and removing his gloves with a pop, "it cost a young man his life, and whoever did this, you *will* be found . . ."

His hands exposed, Cole again picked up the disk. It was oddly cold.

With a deep breath, he placed his thumbs into the depressions. At once, he heard an odd sound in his head, a buzz that reverberated through his skull. Startled, he yanked his hands away, dropping the disk. The buzzing instantly stopped. The artifact clattered to the tabletop and came to rest.

"Enough!" he said, more frightened than he wanted to admit.

Cole backed away from the table and removed his goggles. He crossed to the phone, picked up the receiver, and pressed a button.

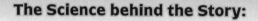

The Science behind the Story:

How Old Is This Place, Anyway?

In "Buried Secrets," Shane Johnson spins an adventure of time travel, fossil hunting, and a big secret buried not in the ground but in a safe. That big secret: the world turns out to be very young, contrary to what our main character believes.

For thousands of years, Christians have debated how old the earth and universe really are. Genesis says God created everything in six days and rested on the seventh. The debate begins with the word *yom*, the Hebrew word for *day*, which is the same word for an age or a long period of time. So the question is, if God took six twenty-four-hour days, then the world must be very young, six thousand to ten thousand years old, right? Or did he use six ages, meaning the world could be ancient, billions of years old?

Many leaders of the early church believed a *day* in the Bible meant a regular day like we have now. They pointed to how Genesis mentions day and night and numbers each day. Other leaders like Justin Martyr, Origen, Iraneus, Thomas Aquinas, Augustine, and John Calvin warned against seeing the Genesis creation as a literal week. They, and others, pointed to Genesis 2:4, which says, "the *day* that the LORD God made the earth and the heavens" (KJV), and they say the word *day* here means the whole creation week. (In any case, all these folks agreed the Bible is to be trusted completely as the Word of God, and they saw science as a friend of faith, a way of trying to figure out how the Creator did his creating.)

The truth is the creation of the universe is a mystery. It happened before anyone was around to write about it, and whatever megaforce gave birth to all things also wiped out any evidence of itself with, er, a bang!

Our layer-cake earth can tell a lot about the unfolding history of the world, but the record in the rocks only stretches back to an age shortly after the beginning. So the debate continues. Whether we use chemistry, astronomy, tree rings, coral reef layers, or ice cores, many scientists insist these yardsticks indicate an earth of great age. And those who believe in a young universe insist God can create things to look old—not to throw us off but so things operate well from the beginning. (For example, he created Adam and Eve as adults so they could survive.)

Interestingly, there are similarities in both points of view. The big bang theory says that in the beginning, there was nothing—no time or physical space—then suddenly the universe came into existence. Christians point to how the Bible describes the event in language hauntingly like the cosmologists': God called the universe into being, saying, "Let there be light."

Why do Christians argue so much about the meaning of a single word like *yom*? For the same reason that the fossil hunter treasures each chunk of bone. Each one tells a tale about the creature it came from and how it lived. Like those old bones, each important part of the Bible must be studied, picked apart, then put back together and studied as a whole. To the person of faith, the Bible is a message from beyond our universe, spoken by the Creator of all things for all people. It is a message without flaw, perfectly communicated. Each word is important.

The age of the earth is not one of those important things about our faith that's essential to salvation. When it comes to opinions of other things, God is more interested in how much we love him and how we live out that love every day. As Micah 6:8 says in the Bible, we are to "act justly and to love mercy and to walk humbly" with our God. That means being patient with other Christians' beliefs, no matter how different they are from ours—agreeing to disagree on matters of opinion and parting as brothers and sisters in Christ, still friends. Christian researcher Roger Wiens says this well: "It is more important to agree on the Rock of Ages than on the age of rocks."

As the dial tone sounded, he paused.

Who would I call?

He glanced at the clock.

Three in the morning—who do I drag out of bed?

He glared at the disk.

Who do I want to know about this when I'm not even sure what I'm dealing with?

Gathering his wits, he returned the phone to its cradle and again approached the table. With each passing moment, his fear was replaced more and more by scientific curiosity.

"Fine, then," he spoke to the object, "we'll go for broke."

He took a seat and picked up the thing. His thumbs again made contact.

The buzzing began, then stopped. He heard a faint whistle like wind whipping through the tunnels of a cave, but he could tell it wasn't his ears that were registering the sound—his mind was receiving a signal directly.

There came a voice. Distant, as if echoing along an impressive length of steel pipe.

"I hope this works," it said.

Cole, astonished, removed one thumb from the disk. The sound stopped at once.

"I'm completing a circuit," he realized.

There was no going back. He had to know.

He renewed his grip.

"I hope this works," the voice repeated. "I don't know who you are or when you'll find this . . . but I marked the disk and its casing, so if you read and understood that, you should be able to understand what I'm saying now. I know it's a one in a trillion shot that this will be found at all . . . a message in a bottle . . ."

The professor closed his eyes, his brow furrowed. Something in the distorted voice rang familiar.

"I don't know how long I have, so I'm going to try to tell you the most important things first. My name is Jacob Larson— "

Surprised, Cole broke contact.

"What *is* this?" he demanded, glaring into the face of the skeleton on his table. His voice was tinged with bewilderment and even anger.

Again he picked up the disk. The initial words played again.

" . . . and I was a paleontology student at the end of the twentieth century. While on a dig, we found something strange . . . a human skeleton in strata much too old to hold such remains. At least, it sure *looked* human. But that wasn't all. Maybe twenty yards away, lodged in an outcropping, I spotted something else . . ."

"Jacob," Cole uttered, the breath torn from him.

". . . a thing of metal, embedded in the rock. I touched it, and there came a flash and a sensation of falling . . . and the next thing I knew, I was . . . somewhere else."

"Where, my boy?" the professor quietly pleaded, his voice quivering. "You have to tell me—"

"Around me was some kind of circular chamber, a place of shining metal and polished crystal. The thing I had touched was still before me, but now on a pedestal of some kind. I was in pain, with burns on my arms and face . . . I could smell my singed hair. And then people rushed into the room . . . huge people . . . dressed like nothing I've ever seen before, speaking a language I'd never heard. Their voices were booming and horrible. They seized me and took me to another room and began to perform medical tests on me . . . at least, I think they were medical tests. Experiments."

Cole stared absently at the disk as it spoke within him.

"They then used images and symbols in an attempt to establish communication with me . . . to get information from me. It became an interrogation . . . I'm pretty sure they were trying to figure out exactly where I came from. It's taken weeks, but I think they know now. And conversely, I've also pieced together where I am, and what happened to me . . ."

"Tell me," Cole whispered, speaking to the absent boy.

"I'm on Earth, but in the distant past."

"Incredible," the professor said, barely aloud. "Could the legends of Atlantis be true . . . ?"

"I saw a map. The land mass here is still a single giant continent . . . Pangaea, we called it in my time. Bears out the theory of continental drift, but the time scale must have been different . . . the drift must have been much more rapid than we ever dreamed. And the civilization here is very high tech, but it's based in natural things, like crystals and glass and metals and ceramics. Almost no plastics at all, from what I've seen. And their woodworking skills are extraordinary. I'm looking right now at interior architecture that blows anything we ever accomplished right out of the water. They've apparently created and mastered composite wood materials that are stronger than steel but much lighter . . ."

Cole fought to visualize it all.

"And the animal life here . . . there are dinosaurs! Right before my own eyes, I've seen them . . . so many sizes and colors, and they don't look the way we thought they did. So hard to describe . . . and these people don't think any more of them than we think of elephants or giraffes or anything else. And they have those too, by the way

. . . all species of animals, all phyla, all living at the same time. Dinosaurs and mammals and birds and fish . . . everything! Wide-scale evolution never took place . . . every kind of creature coexisted from the outset. I wish I could tell Professor Cole . . ."

Cole, shaken at that, dropped his head.

"But the most surprising thing is that, from what I've been able to gather, I'm not millions of years in the past, or even hundreds of thousands, but only several thousand, based on the time-line diagrams they've shown me. My mom was right . . . I thought she was silly to have taken the Genesis account in the Bible so literally, but she was right. I've always believed in God, but I guess I also believed a little too much in man and in what he takes for science . . .

"I wish I could learn more here . . . I wish I could understand their language. But it's so complex, and they're so impatient. It makes it hard to communicate when you can't really ask questions . . ."

After a pause, the voice went on.

"This place . . . these people . . . it's like some kind of hell. They're devils, all of them! You can see that they're brilliant of mind, but they're also wicked and utterly without compassion. Torture and slavery is rampant here . . . cruelty like I've never seen. Every face is scarred. They fight constantly with each other . . . I don't know how they get anything accomplished. Life has no value here."

Cole shuddered in horror.

"They seem to relish the inflicting of pain . . . It's almost like an art. The torments I've seen in my short time here . . . Some of the captives have had horrible things done to them. Unspeakable things. So far, they've kept me alive . . . They must be studying me, but when they've finished, who knows what will happen. They seem to have performed some kind of surgery on me. Cut me across the middle . . . Who knows what they did. I've been kept in a cell nearly the whole time . . . I've been given water and some kind of bread but not much else . . ."

There was a pause. Cole heard shouts in the background—strange, unearthly cries in deep and menacing voices.

"But only minutes ago," Jacob finally went on, "something drew their attention away from the detention area . . . I don't know what. They went running, leaving open the door to my cell. I slipped out and found this handheld notation machine, and I hope I'm working it right . . . I've watched them make recordings on it so many times. They use it to file reports on me . . . At least, that's what I think they were doing . . ."

The professor wanted to speak to Jacob, but no words would come.

More shouts. Sounds of a distant scuffle, of movement, of hurried motion. A prolonged silence followed. Finally Jacob resumed his narrative, but more quietly.

"That was close. I'm now in hiding inside a small storage cubicle . . . I pray they don't hear me . . ."

Cole, tears flooding his eyes, wanted to reach back, to rescue his esteemed assistant—but there was nothing to be done. His grip on the disk tightened. He grew angry at his helplessness.

"Since I got here, I've been trying to figure out what happened to me . . . trying to form a theory, given what I know. The thing I touched, the thing that brought me here . . . It must have been some kind of time travel experiment. I suppose it had been buried for all those millennia but somehow remained active. When I touched it, I must have set it off and it homed on its point of origin, carrying me back here with it. I don't think these people expected to see me . . . didn't expect the thing to transport a person across the centuries like that. I don't know. They seemed surprised and delighted, as if this opened up whole new possibilities for them . . ."

Another pause. Cole, without realizing, held his breath.

"If these people were to have access to the course of time, I shudder to think of the damage they could do. I mean, the catastrophe they could unleash on the world, against the different ages of man! They could destroy history as we know it and wipe out virtually all of humanity. Who knows what they're capable of, but if they can do this . . ."

More strange voices, rising and falling as if running past.

"There must be some way to destroy that device . . . to stop them . . ."

The words ceased, though the background echo continued. Then sounds of further movement. Cole listened intently, straining to hear.

"Speak to me, Jacob," he whispered. "Please . . ."

After several suspenseful moments, the report went on.

"I'm moving down a corridor now . . . The hallways, the chambers all appear to be deserted. There are a few shouts coming from back in the area of the holding cells . . . prisoners, I think, still locked up . . . but otherwise, nothing. No voices, no sounds of movement . . . no sign of my captors."

An agonizing, lingering stretch of quiet.

"There's a door up ahead," the student said, excitement filling his voice. "Looks like some kind of daylight . . . I think it leads outside. Maybe I can get away . . ."

The words ceased. Cole shut his eyes and wordlessly pleaded Jacob to continue. Suddenly a steady roar resonated within him. When the voice again spoke, it was all but swallowed up in the din.

"I'm outside now. No sign of anyone. Very windy. It's starting to rain . . . coming down hard now . . . I can barely see. I've got to find a place to take cover . . ."

"Jacob . . ."

"I hear screams all around me . . . You'd think they'd never seen rain before. There's thunder in the distance . . . a deep, continuous rumble. Never heard anything like it. Wait, yes, I have! At Niagara Falls, summer before last. Water! It's getting louder . . . closer . . . The ground's starting to shake . . ."

The roar, the screams increased to a terrifying level.

"Genesis . . . the flood of Noah . . . It all makes sense now! I've got to stop recording . . . going to seal this disk in its casing and try to secure it under my shirt. Whoever is hearing this, you have to tell the world what I've seen . . . They have to know! Truth above all . . ."

The disk went silent. Utterly, ominously silent.

"Jacob!" Cole cried out, as if to force a reply. A thumb momentarily slipped from its place, then slid back into the still-warm oval.

"I hope this works," the account began again. "I don't know who you are or when you'll find this . . ."

In shock, Cole released the disk. It dropped hard onto the table, spun like a coin, and came to rest. He glanced over at the bottom of the metal container as it sat askew atop the block of stone and at the odd material lining it. For the first time, he noticed a layer of moisture where the disk had rested.

Rainwater, Cole realized, dipping a finger into the wetness.

"Genesis," he said, the word soaked in dread.

He pushed back from the worktable. In horror, his gaze

fell upon the skeleton, upon the grinning skull staring up at him.

Jacob. He now knew.

"No," he said, refusing to believe it all. "It's impossible."

Cole staggered back, knocking his chair over, barely keeping his balance. His eyes never left the convicting skull.

"It can't be."

He turned and moved away, covering his face with his hands, trembling, desperately wanting not to believe.

But something within him did.

"How . . . *how* . . . ?"

He dropped hard into a plush armchair near the fire. His breath came in dry, greedy gulps as his heart flew against his chest. His arms and legs quivered. He felt as if he had run ten miles.

The hours slipped past. Morning light began to rise, flowing coldly through the frost-tinged glass of the towering windows.

Cole awoke with a start, realizing only then that he had fallen asleep. A few of the whitened embers in the fireplace still glowed a dull red. Feeling the solidity of the leather chair beneath him, he spread his fingers and rubbed its arms hard, embracing reality.

"A dream," he whispered hopefully, rubbing his eyes, his face. He filled his lungs, forced the air out sharply, and rose awkwardly to his feet. He glanced at the antique clock atop the mantle. Its pendulum swung steadily, its ticking the only sound in the room.

"After seven," he noted, running a hand through his thinning hair.

He spun toward the worktable. The toppled chair lay on the floor. Stepping closer, he looked fearfully at the sedimentary slab, not wanting to find what waited there.

The skeleton, still largely trapped in the stone.

The casing, open and empty.

The disk, now quiet.

The disk.

It had been real. All of it.

Cole, coming to terms with hard truth, walked up to the table. As he neared, a tiny something caught the snow-filtered daylight, capturing his attention. Pushing the swing-arm lamp out of his way, he leaned over and picked up one of the encrusted fingers he had removed the night before.

He had missed something then—a glint of gold, shining out through a crack in the stone.

Cole pried the fissure open, splitting the hardened covering cleanly along the fault, to reveal bone encircled by metal.

A sound of sorrow spilled from his throat.

Jacob's high school ring, he thought, turning the discolored jewelry in his fingers. There was no doubt—the blue gem, the graduation date, and the tiny raised cross engraved along the side all cried out to him. Even the young man's first name was there, plainly visible in block letters.

Poor boy. Poor, poor boy . . .

Gently he set bone back in place against the hand from which it had come and did the same with the other digits he had removed.

"I'm sorry, son," Cole said to the remains before him, his eyes wet, his hands shaking. "I'm so sorry."

He picked up the disk and its casing and stood there for a long time, his mind struggling like an animal in a trap. Carefully he slipped the recording back into its container, replaced the lid, and gave it a gentle twist. He heard a momentary hiss as once again the object sealed itself against the ages.

For a long time, Cole just stood there holding the object, considering with great sadness the fossilized remains of his assistant.

"I'm sorry, Jacob," he repeated.

With newfound resolve, the weary professor again picked up the finger bone around which the ring was locked.

Forgive me . . .

Slowly and almost reverently, he turned and walked across the room. He halted before the large, framed plaque, the one to which he had pointed through the years, the one that had served class after class, year after year, as a cherished guidepost of scientific integrity. Lifting it from its hook and placing it aside, he revealed, for the first time in a very long time, a small, concealed wall safe.

Cole had to pause to recall the combination. In moments, with a creak, the door was open. Into the dark chamber beyond he tenderly placed the casing with its miraculous disk and the finger bone with its now ancient ring. The scientist within him couldn't bear the thought of their destruction, but neither could their existence be shared with the world. Far too much was at stake—were they to be revealed, the foundation of established science would irrevocably be shaken, the pillars of accepted knowledge toppled, and the works of great scientific minds the world over revealed as error.

I'm so very sorry.

With wet eyes, he closed the door and locked it tight. As he returned the plaque to its place of honor, again he read its inscription: "Truth above All."

The words haunted him, and they would for the rest of his life. Haunted him in Jacob's voice.

He contemplated the skeleton on the table. He didn't yet know what excuse he would give for its disappearance, but he would think of something. The boy deserved a decent burial at least, albeit in secret.

No one, Cole knew, could ever know whose remains they had found—just as no one else would ever hear the last words of a brave young man, recorded for the ages.

Dropping more wood onto the grate, he renewed the fire. Blazing brightly once again, it was as a funeral pyre—and into the flames went the evidence recorded by the camera, which had seen all. Dark, acrid smoke rose as the videocassettes melted and burned, floating away up the chimney as fumes and ash and soot.

The shattered mentor went to the window and stared out at the bleak, frozen world beyond. The barren, windwhipped trees, the untouched snow, the shadowy sky above—all remained the same.

And yet, for Martin Cole, now and forever, they had changed.

Talismort's hub was full of fascinating artifacts. I made my way along the curving counter and inspected things under glass, on stands, and locked inside clear cabinets.

I was looking at a small, silver gadget on the shelf next to the Mars rocks when Amy screamed. She was standing by the open door of a cabinet across the hub. A toneless voice came from within the darkened closet.

"I am sorry if I have disturbed you in any—you in any—you in any—*bleep*."

A man leaned out of the cabinet and stood up. At least, I thought it was a man at first. But his skin was metallic, and his eyes flashed with an orange glow.

Talismort waved his arms as he hurried across the room. "Have no fear, my dear. It's only a robot. A servebot. A broken one, at that."

The robot retreated into a sitting position. His orange, glowing eyes dimmed and faded to darkness. The servebot slumped, as if he were napping.

"Oh," Amy wheezed. "Good. Only a robot. I thought it was a real person." She was catching her breath, trying to look casual. She tapped the sleeping chest of the mechanical man. "Just a bucket of bolts."

The flat voice came out of the cabinet again. "Bucket of b—bucket of—buck—*boing*."

Talismort seemed hurt for a moment, but he quickly recovered his good nature. "A bucket of bolts? Just wire and gears and electronic impulses, yes?"

Neither of us answered. We knew something was up.

"You might be surprised, even shocked, at what a simple bucket of bolts like this can do!" Talismort patted the robot's shoulder. "This bucket, for example, is called Proteus. He had a twin brother named Tin Man. Tin Man was quite remarkable, not for how he was made but for what he did."

Tin Man

Jim Denney

The boy awoke with a startled cry.

Tin Man hovered over him, staring with glowing red eyes.

The boy turned away. "What are you looking at, Tin Man?" he asked.

"You cried out in your sleep, Jobe," Tin Man replied in a flat, electronic voice. Tin Man was a servebot, a machine in the shape of a man.

"Get outta my face, will you?" Jobe said. He placed both hands against Tin Man's chest and shoved. The chrome-steel servebot floated backward in the zero gravity of the escape capsule.

"Something in your dream made you afraid," Tin Man said. "What were you dreaming about, Jobe?" The servebot's body thumped against the padding of the far wall and rebounded.

"I don't remember," Jobe said.

Tin Man knew the boy was lying. Jobe's face was slick with sweat, and the bot's sensitive audio sensors could hear the boy's heart pounding against his ribcage.

"Was it the same dream you have had before, Jobe?" Tin Man asked. "Was it the dream where you are floating among the stars and you cannot breathe because there is no air?"

Jobe didn't answer.

Tin Man gazed steadily at Jobe. The boy looked so thin and miserable with his large, sad eyes, his hollow cheeks, his thin slash of a mouth, and his ragged mop of soot-black hair. He wore a short-sleeved orange jumpsuit. The chocolate-brown skin of his thin arms was marked by puckered scars, evidence of a harsh life.

"Jobe, are you sure you do not remember your dream?" the servebot asked. "You might feel better if you talk about it."

"Shut up and leave me alone!" Jobe snapped, unbuckling the straps that bound him to the acceleration couch. "And quit staring at me! Those red eyes of yours really creep me out!"

Jobe's couch was on the right side of the tiny sphere-shaped capsule; the servebot's couch was on the left. After removing the restraining straps, Jobe climbed through the narrow gap between the two acceleration couches and eased himself weightlessly into the small space at the rear of the capsule.

"I am sorry you are annoyed by the glow from my visual receptors, Jobe," Tin Man said. "Chaplain Potter ordered me to watch you at all times."

"Yeah?" Jobe said, sneering. "Well, you don't have to

take orders from Chaplain Potter anymore. He's dead—like everyone else on that starship."

"I think he survived," the bot replied. "There was over a minute of warning before the *Regulus* exploded. I am sure the entire crew got away safely—including Chaplain Potter."

The magnets in the soles of Jobe's ankle socks clanked against the airlock door at the rear of the capsule, holding Jobe in place. He slid a cabinet door open. Inside the cabinet was a device made of hoses, wires, and a funnel—the zero-gravity toilet. Jobe used the toilet, then pressed a button that flushed it with a whoosh of compressed air. The nozzle of the decontaminator hissed, and a puff of spray cooled his hands. Jobe rubbed his hands together, then closed the cabinet.

"If Chaplain Potter is in an escape capsule right now," the boy said, "he's probably wondering the same thing I am—'How long till the air runs out?'"

"You should not talk that way, Jobe," Tin Man said. "You are only fourteen. You have your whole life ahead of you. The rescue ships are searching. There is always a chance they will find us."

"A chance?" Jobe said, laughing bitterly. "What are the odds anyone will find us, Tin Man? A million to one?" The boy tugged his magnet soles off the airlock door and floated free.

"I admit that a rescue seems unlikely," the bot said.

Jobe drifted toward the storage locker, opened it, and sipped from the water-dispensing tube. He took a zip pack of protein squares from the storage bin and closed the locker. Then he pulled himself through the gap between the couches.

"We've been out here thirteen days, Tin Man," the boy said, hovering over his couch. "Face it, nobody's looking for us. And even if they were, they'd never find us. We have no radio, no distress beacon, nothing to signal with. The only piece of equipment that still works on this capsule is the proximity detector—and a lot of help *that* is! If a rescue ship does happen to sail by, we can detect them, but they can't detect us."

"Still," Tin Man said, "we must not give up hope." The servebot settled onto the left-hand acceleration couch and buckled the restraints.

"I quit hoping a long time ago, Tin Man," Jobe said. "I'm not scared of dying. I'm not scared of nothing." He settled himself onto the right-hand couch and pulled the straps over his shoulders and waist. "Besides, from what you told me, this what-do-you-call-it, this hypocrisy thing—"

"You mean hypoxia?"

"Yeah, hypoxia—lack of oxygen." He opened the zip pack and began munching on a protein square. "It doesn't sound like such a bad way to go. Didn't you tell me you just get dizzy and you don't even know what's happening?"

Tin Man could see the rapid pulse in the carotid artery of Jobe's neck. Though the boy claimed not to be, he was scared—very scared.

"Jobe," the servebot said, "I am just a machine. You do not need to act brave around me."

Jobe shrugged and looked away. He finished eating the first protein square, then took the second square from the zip pack. "I used to help make this stuff, you know," he said, "back on Gamma Gruesome."

"Gamma Gruesome?" the bot asked.

"My home planet," Jobe said, crunching a bite. "It's really called Gamma Gruis Four, but everybody who lives there calls it Gamma Gruesome, the armpit of the galaxy. There's nothing on that planet but swamps and slime beans and bloodworms." He made a sour face. "And Mr. Flint."

"Why were you living with Mr. Flint?" Tin Man asked. "Why did you not live with your parents?"

Jobe shrugged. "I never had any parents. I lived at the state orphanage till I was nine. Then Mr. Flint came and took me home with him. He made me work on his farm, harvesting Dhanabian slime beans."

"Slime beans," Tin Man said. "A highly concentrated source of protein." The bot noticed that Jobe's pulse had settled down a bit. Good. Talking got Jobe's mind off his fears.

"Yeah," Jobe said, holding up the last bit of protein square. "The stuff doesn't taste half bad once it's processed." He popped the bite into his mouth, then talked with his mouth full. "But when those beans are growing in the bog, they stink like rotting meat. At harvesttime, Mr. Flint made me wade in the swamp up to my chest. There's a smell that gets into your skin and stays with you for days." He wrinkled his nose.

"I would not know," Tin Man said. "Bots have no sense of smell. Tell me—how did you get away from Mr. Flint?"

"I ran away," Jobe said. "Several times. First time, I was really dumb. I went straight to the orphanage and begged them not to send me back to Mr. Flint. So what did they do? They called him and had him come get me. Mr. Flint really worked me over after that."

The servebot's red eyes flickered. "He *beat* you? I am sorry to hear that, Jobe."

The boy's face hardened. "I didn't care," he said with a shrug. "Flint didn't scare me. He could hit me all he wanted, I wasn't scared." Tin Man noticed the pulse pounding in the boy's neck again.

"I kept running away," Jobe continued. "Flint kept

catching me. One day, I stole some money from Flint and hopped a swamp skimmer that was hauling protein to Gammaport. I used the money to bribe a guy at the loading bay. He sneaked me into a cargo container that was headed for a star freighter, the *Regulus*."

"Was he the man who gave you the meteorite?" the servebot asked.

"You mean this rock?" Jobe reached into a pocket of his jumpsuit and pulled out a cube shaped stone. "Yeah. When I handed him the money to hide me in the container, he gave me this rock. He told me spacemen carry space rocks for luck. He said a stowaway on a star freighter would need plenty of luck. Then he closed up the container, and the transport hauled the container, with me in it, up to the *Regulus*."

"May I see the meteorite?" the servebot asked.

Jobe shrugged and tossed the gray rock. It sailed straight into Tin Man's open hand. Jobe had good aim.

"Belief in luck is a common human superstition," Tin Man said, examining the rock. "This is nothing but a common meteorite, Jobe—an iron crystal called an octahedrite. This piece of space debris will not bring you luck." The bot tossed the meteorite back to Jobe.

"It sure hasn't so far," Jobe replied grimly, tucking the space stone back in his pocket. "I guess it would take a lot more than luck to save a messed-up loser like me. Just look at my life—born on the worst planet in the galaxy, no parents, growing up in the swamps with the bloodworms feeding on me every day—" His voice choked, and he swore bitterly.

"Jobe, please do not—"

"I finally got away from that stinking swamp planet— and what happens? The starship blows up! Now I'm sitting in this cramped little capsule, waiting for the air to run out. I was born a loser, Tin Man. I guess I'll die a loser."

Jobe's bitter words triggered Tin Man's molecular memory—a memory of the day the servebot first met Jobe . . .

Chaplain Potter had sent Tin Man to the galley to get a dinner from the food dispenser. The servebot found the boy hiding under a table, his pockets crammed with stolen food. Tin Man took Jobe by the arm and dragged him to Chaplain Potter. The chaplain didn't want the boy to spend the rest of the voyage sitting in the brig, so he accepted responsibility for the young stowaway.

The starship never reached its destination. Seventeen days after leaving orbit around Gamma Gruis Four, disaster struck. Late in the third watch, as the star freighter *Regulus* cruised through hyperspace, Tin Man was with Jobe in the conditioning room.

As the boy exercised on the resistance machine, Chaplain Potter rushed in, waving a sheet of faxfilm. The Chaplain was a white-haired man with merry eyes and ruddy cheeks. "Jobe," he said, "I just got a starfax from Interstellar Command. They checked out your Mr. Flint, and it turns out he's a very bad man—wanted on three planets. They have him under arrest."

"Does this mean I don't have to go back to him?" Jobe said.

"That's right," the chaplain said. "When we get to Ankor Edge, you'll start a new life. You can—"

Chaplain Potter didn't get to finish his sentence, for at that very moment, an alarm shrieked—the most nerve-jangling sound ever heard by a human ear. It signaled the unthinkable: antimatter containment failure.

The ship's antimatter fuel required constant magnetic containment. If antimatter and normal matter ever came into contact, the entire starship would vanish in an explosion far greater than a thermonuclear blast. Containment failures on starships were rare, almost unheard of—but when they happened, there was very little warning. Once the alarm sounded, everyone aboard had no more than a minute to find an escape capsule and abandon ship.

"What's happening?" Jobe shouted over the wailing alarm.

A shudder passed through the ship. *Regulus* had dropped out of hyperspace. Stranded in normal space, hundreds of millions of miles from the nearest star system, *Regulus* transmitted a distress signal by hypercommunicator.

Along the outer wall of the conditioning room, escape doors slid open.

"Tin Man!" Chaplain Potter shouted. "Get Jobe to an escape capsule! Stay with him and get clear of the ship!"

"You should go with the boy," Tin Man said.

"I'll take another capsule," the chaplain said. "You stay with Jobe. Bots don't use oxygen—Jobe will have twice as much air to breathe if you stay with him! Now go!"

Tin Man pulled Jobe to one of the open escape doors, pushed the boy through, then followed. The boy and the bot tumbled into the escape capsule together. The inner and outer airlock doors hissed shut behind them.

Working with machinelike efficiency, Tin Man strapped Jobe into one of the two acceleration couches, grabbed one of the handholds along the wall, and pressed the launch button. The escape capsule fired into empty space at an acceleration of eight g's.

"What happens now?" Jobe asked, barely able to speak.

"Brace yourself," Tin Man answered.

Seconds later, it came—

A blast that rattled Jobe's teeth and clattered Tin Man's steel joints. The walls of the capsule screamed as waves of superheated plasma blasted by—a firestorm of ions, electrons, and subatomic particles. The sound and terror seemed to go on and on.

Then came the most frightening sound of all: silence.

Hours passed. Tin Man tried to make radio contact with other escape capsules, but the radio didn't work. The distress beacon was also broken.

Finally Tin Man went out through the airlock and inspected the charred, pitted hull of the capsule. Where the radio and beacon transmitter should have been, Tin Man found only blobs of metal that had melted, then cooled and hardened. The only electronic device not destroyed by the explosion was the proximity detector, located on the forward section of the hull.

Thirteen days had gone by since the destruction of the *Regulus*. The capsule's limited supply of oxygen was running out.

"Jobe," Tin Man said, "if Chaplain Potter were here, he would make a suggestion regarding our predicament."

"What suggestion?" the boy said.

"He would tell us to pray."

"Is that supposed to be funny?" Jobe sneered.

"Bots do not joke," Tin Man said.

"Well, then you've got a screw loose, Tin Man! You know what praying is? It's talking to somebody who doesn't exist!"

"But Chaplain Potter said—"

"Potter tried to cram his religion down my throat," Jobe said. "He told me some crazy story about a guy named Jesus. Some people killed him; then three days later, he was walking around alive again. What a bunch of—"

"I have heard the chaplain talk about Jesus," Tin Man said, "and I know he is convinced that Jesus is alive. If that is so, then Jesus is the very person we should talk to, because he solved the death problem—the very problem we are facing now."

"You're crazier than Old Man Potter," Jobe said, eyes wide with disbelief.

"I am being perfectly rational," Tin Man replied. "Praying is your only logical option. After all, if you pray and Jesus is not alive to hear your prayer, then you are no worse off than if you had not prayed. But if he hears you and saves you from death, then your situation is greatly improved. So, logically, you have nothing to lose and everything to gain by praying."

"Look!" Jobe snarled. "I don't need some mindless bucket of bolts telling me to pray! Just shut up, will you?"

Tin Man's glowing eyes dimmed in surprise. "That is an irrational response. Perhaps your fear of dying has—"

"I told you!" Jobe said. "I'm not scared of dying! I'm not scared of nothing!"

Again Tin Man noticed the rapid throbbing of the boy's pulse.

"If you will not pray," the servebot said, "then I will pray for you."

"I don't want you praying for me either," Jobe said.

"My programming requires that I do everything I can to prevent you from being harmed, Jobe," Tin Man answered. "If there is even a slight possibility that a bot's prayers can be heard, then I must pray for you."

Tin Man wasn't sure how to begin. Chaplain Potter had always prayed with his eyes closed. Tin Man's glowing red visual receptors went dark. "Jesus," Tin Man said, "I am only a machine, but please hear my prayer—"

"Shut up, Tin Man!" Jobe warned. "Stop praying!"

"Please permit this boy to be rescued. And if you will not rescue him, at least help him not to be afraid when—"

Smash!

Something struck Tin Man in the face. The bot turned on both visual receptors—but only one of them was working. The right eye was dead and sightless. With its good left eye, the servebot saw little pieces of glittering debris floating in the air—fragments of a shattered robotic eye. Spinning among the little red eye fragments was something gray and roughly cube shaped. Tin Man grabbed it—Jobe's lucky meteorite.

Tin Man looked at Jobe. The boy's face was twisted in rage.

"I told you, Tin Man!" Jobe shouted. "Don't pray for me! I don't need help from anyone! Especially not from some dead man who doesn't exist! I'm not scared to die! I'm not scared of—"

One teardrop trembled at the lower edge of Jobe's right eye. Then it floated weightlessly, like a bubble, shimmering in midair.

"Help me, Tin Man!" the boy said in a voice suddenly small and tight with fear. "I don't want to die! I don't want to—" He choked up.

Tin Man slipped free of the couch restraints and floated over to Jobe. The boy stared in horror at the dark, empty socket where the bot's right eye had been. "I—I'm sorry, Tin Man! I didn't mean to hurt you!" Jobe unbuckled his restraints, flung his arms around Tin Man, and clung tightly.

The Science behind the Story

Build Your Own Droid

Every few years, we change the way we think of robots. It usually depends on what's popular in the theaters or in the latest sci-fi story. From the original tin man in *The Wizard of Oz* to C-3PO and R2-D2 in *Star Wars* . . . and beyond.

But what about real robots? Today, police use remote-controlled robots to help unplug bombs. Archaeologists use robots to explore shipwrecks and find lost treasures in places humans can't go. Kids even build their own robots with science kits and join robot clubs that compete against each other.

But when most of us think of robots, we think of space. And real space robots are on their way too! NASA scientists are developing a softball-size floating robot for the International Space Station. These PSAs, or personal satellite assistants, could ferry information back and forth between astronauts, pass out information like floating encyclopedias, or even sniff the air to make sure it's safe to breathe—which is important if you can't step outside for a breath of fresh air.

So robots have crossed the line from fantasy to reality. You may have a robot cleaning your swimming pool or mowing your lawn sometime soon. Still, bots may not ever truly possess AI, or artificial intelligence. A computer program *mimics* what humans do, but it doesn't have its own thoughts, actions, or awareness like a human being. And the more scientists learn about how hard it is to create an artificial intelligence, the more amazing our natural, God-created intelligence becomes.

Still, it would be cool if bots understood that faith makes sense, like Tin Man in our story. After all, isn't *not* believing illogical?

"You did not hurt me, Jobe," the servebot said, hugging the boy gently with arms that could bend steel.

"I'm so scared, Tin Man," Jobe said. "After this is over, please don't tell anyone I was scared. I don't want anyone to know."

"I will tell everyone how brave you were," Tin Man said.

"Your skin is cold," the boy said.

"I am sorry," Tin Man said.

"It's okay," the boy said. He clung to Tin Man and sobbed. Several more teardrops floated on the air. Minutes passed. Finally Jobe fell silent. Tin Man checked the boy's face.

Jobe was asleep—no, not asleep. Unconscious. His lips were blue, and his breathing was labored. Was it oxygen starvation? Was the capsule running out of air sooner than expected?

Tin Man settled the boy's limp body onto the couch and strapped him in. Jobe's eyes fluttered open. "Tin Man?" he said weakly.

"Just rest," the servebot said. "Everything is all right."

Jobe closed his eyes.

After a few minutes, he began breathing normally. Apparently, his emotional strain had caused him to use up oxygen too quickly. There was no doubt about it—the capsule's air supply was failing. There was probably no more than an hour of oxygen remaining.

Tin Man's one red eye went dark. "Jesus," the bot said, "if you can hear me, Jobe needs your help right now."

Blip!

Tin Man turned and looked with one good eye in the direction of the sound. The blip had come from the proximity detector.

Blip!

The proximity detector was set into the console on the

forward bulkhead, directly in front of the two couches. Tin Man drifted closer and checked the detector's glowing blue screen. It showed an object coming into range—a heavy starship, judging from its motion and gravity signature. It was still a few hundred thousand miles away and moving slowly.

Exactly as a search-and-rescue ship would move.

Blip!

On its present course, the starship would come fairly close to the escape capsule—within twenty thousand miles. But without a distress signal, the searchers would never know the capsule was there.

Blip!

Floating weightlessly, Tin Man turned and looked at Jobe, asleep on the acceleration couch. Tin Man opened the metal hand that still gripped the shiny gray rock—Jobe's lucky meteorite.

Blip!

Working quickly, using one sharp corner of the meteorite as a writing tool, Tin Man scratched letters into the painted metal console. With mechanical precision, the bot wrote four neat lines of words above the glowing blue screen of the proximity detector.

Blip!

Done.

Tin Man checked Jobe one last time, then went to the rear of the capsule, opened the inner door, and stepped into the airlock. It took thirty seconds for the airlock to cycle. Tin Man opened the outer door and crawled onto the charred skin of the capsule, gripping the external handholds. The airlock door slid silently shut.

The servebot looked about with one eye. All around, the stars gleamed with a steady light. Directly overhead, the Milky Way splashed the sky with a heavenly light.

Tin Man released the handholds and slowly drifted away from the capsule. The bot couldn't speak because there is no sound in space. Still, Tin Man's molecular logic processor could generate one final, peaceful thought: *Thank you.*

Then, with one hand, the bot pried open and removed its steel chest plate and cast it off into space. In the other hand, the bot held the iron meteorite.

Within Tin Man's chest cavity, in the place where the heart would be in a human being, was the power nexus. A crack in the shielding of the nexus would trigger a powerful explosion. Tin Man gripped the meteorite and calculated the amount of force that would be needed. The metal arm swung like a sledgehammer, driving the meteorite into the power nexus.

Light exploded silently in airless space.

The explosion unleashed a broadband, high-intensity burst of electrons and photoelectrons—an electromagnetic pulse. The pulse expanded outward. In less than two seconds, the pulse reached the approaching starship and sent a surge of current through the ship's electronic systems. Within moments, the crew of the starship located the source of the electromagnetic pulse and changed course to investigate—just as Tin Man had planned.

Inside the escape capsule, the hull rang like a bell. Jobe was startled awake. His head hurt. It was hard to breathe. At the edge of his awareness, a sound kept repeating: *Blip!* . . . *Blip!* . . . *Blip!*

Jobe unbuckled the straps that held him on the acceleration couch. He looked around the capsule. "Tin Man!" he called. "Tin Man!"

No answer.

Jobe arose from the acceleration couch and floated toward the proximity detector—and he gasped. A ship was approaching!

Blip! . . . Blip! . . . Blip!

There were words scratched into the painted metal above the screen. Jobe began reading—then his vision blurred. He wiped his eyes and read the words again:

JOBE, YOU HAVE A NEW LIFE.

IT IS A GIFT. USE IT WELL.

YOUR FRIEND,

TIN MAN

When Talismort got going, his stories were mesmerizing. There we sat, still in the station's hub, feeling like we had traveled the galaxy. Amy walked past the robot's cabinet toward the far wall. She gave the closet a wide berth. I think she was still nervous. But it was obvious that the robot had interrupted her checking out something beyond the cabinet, something she hadn't forgotten about.

She leaned over a container that was crowned by tubes and wires. It seemed to be steaming. She reached toward it, then pulled her hand back as if she'd been burned. "It's cold!"

"Very," Talismort said. "It comes from the frigid edge of our solar system, out where the birth of the planets is frozen in time and space."

"Is it . . . ice?" Amy asked.

Talismort nodded.

"A chunk of comet?" I guessed. "I know the Kuiper belt is full of frozen comets and icy asteroids."

"Yes, it's a cold, dark place where the sun is a bright star and day seems as night," Talismort said. He gazed into the jar.

The tubes pumped impossibly cold air into the container. On a little clear stand in the center sat a blue-gray sphere the size of a tennis ball. It was crystal clear, and it scattered light like a diamond. Rainbows spread across the ceiling above it. Deep inside, shapes danced, glowing shapes of things just out of focus. A butterfly? A fire's glowing ember? A dolphin splashing in a deep, blue lagoon?

"There are many stories that ice can tell us," Talismort said. "The ice of comets has been around since the Creator put form to the sun and planets and moons. This ice is from that dark time and place. It's from a comet called Wild 2. A gigantic, floating, cosmic iceberg. Until a few centuries ago, it was a comet that spent most of its life out in the eternal night. It came close to the sun once every few thousand years. But then one of the bigger planets grabbed it and flung it into a shorter orbit. Now it stays close to the inner solar system." He patted the case gently. "But this ice, this relic, came from out there. And the things it has seen might surprise you. Before this piece fell off, the giant ice ball it came from had quite a ride. It had a passenger too. Her name was Ester."

For Such a Time

Robert Elmer

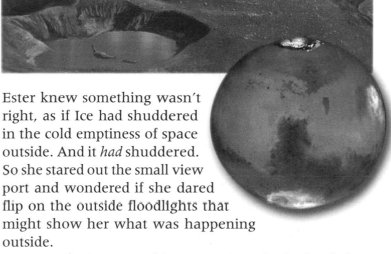

Ester knew something wasn't right, as if Ice had shuddered in the cold emptiness of space outside. And it *had* shuddered. So she stared out the small view port and wondered if she dared flip on the outside floodlights that might show her what was happening outside.

Or maybe it was nothing. Last time she had only lost a small piece, nothing to worry about. But this time felt different. Maybe it wouldn't hurt to light up again.

Of course, Ice would be as it always had been—part of her home world, a giant sphere of pearly blue-white, speckled with drifting space rocks and pebbles it had picked up in the outer reaches of their solar system. She could check, but Ice would look rough cut and comforting, always close but silent as the stars that stared back at her through the opposite port. She reached for the orange button that would light up the giant, dirty snowball their ship had been pushing from the outer reaches for . . .

For how long? As *A-13* shook once more, Ester checked the chrono, but the numbers and the time meant no more to her today than they had when she was a little girl, before Mommy and Daddy had died, before they had left her alone on *A-13* to push Ice. Not that she minded. Or if she did, she had no choice. After all, she belonged to this place, knew every inch of the small control room, the galley, the two crew tubes with sleep pads and the grav tube that spun her three times a day to keeping her muscles working.

No, she didn't mind. This was her home world, and she loved it, loved Ice, loved the Book. But still she wondered sometimes . . .

Daddy, why did you leave me? She asked the framed holo once more, but once more the small 3-D photo on the wall above the main thruster controls would only say what it had always said, what Daddy had programmed there on his last day, a week after Mommy had died.

"I'm so sorry, princess." Her father's face looked up at her, as it had hundreds of times before. His eyes looked hollow, the way they'd looked the day he got sick. It had happened before his six-year-old daughter really knew what was happening. He coughed. "Your mother and I didn't mean for it to happen this way. But the ship will take care of itself. And God will take care of you. I know he has something special for you. So you just read the Book. And hold on, Ester. Hold on."

Oh, she'd held on, all right. One year, then two. Five years, then ten. A long time. No time. She'd read the Book over and over, especially the story with her name at the top, the queen she had been named for. And she remembered the words, though she couldn't say she understood them all. She had a hard time picturing the world the story described, the people who lived in a land of rocky hills and dusty mountains.

Then again, she didn't always understand her own small home world inside *A-13* either—the random flashes of light from the nav controls, the numbers on screens that would never quite make sense to her the way they had to Daddy. Because the numbers, like the words in the Book, never seemed to explain themselves.

Still, it was her home world, the only world she had ever known. It was her place, and her place, she understood, was to protect that world. She knew Daddy had put her in charge for a reason, just like he'd underlined the Verse for a reason. The story of Esther, section four, word group fourteen—"And who knows but that you have come to royal position for such a time as this?" She often kept the Book, the only book she had ever seen, open to that page, stuck to the bulkhead where she could read it as she floated about.

She didn't yet know what kind of time Daddy had meant. But *A-13* pushed on, the way Daddy had told her it would. Only, now she wasn't sure what had happened—especially when she heard the scraping of ice from the front of the hull to the back, like some horrible giant scraping its fingernails along the outside.

"What's that?" she asked herself.

As if to answer, the ship shuddered once more, and Ester screamed when she heard a voice crackling over the overhead speakers—louder than she had ever heard.

Even without checking a sat nav, Edison Wesley could close his eyes and know just where he was, from the deep tracks in the red Martian dust to the rim of Gusev Crater Lake. The *Spirit* rover had set down many years ago, before people had come to live on the red planet, before they'd brought the air and the water that allowed moss and lichen to spread across the surface, before the hardy hairgrass and pearlwort had been genetically modified from specimens taken from the earth's South Pole. He grinned and adjusted the thin breather hose that snaked out of the back of his parka and looped around his face, just under his nose. He was a lot like the Martian grasses that now covered the once-barren landscape: He hung in there. He belonged.

And he didn't take stupid chances like his friend Jaimee.

"You'd better head in, Jaimee." He leaned on the mini rover's com button and scanned the flat surface of the huge crater lake, 150 kilometers across and backed by the southern highlands. "It's only three hours away."

"Hey, there you are, Wes." His friend's voice cracked over the com, not as loud as it could have been, barely loud enough to hear. "Here to see the show?"

"No way. When that thing hits, the wave's probably going to slosh way over the rim. I only came to warn you."

"Yeah, that's sweet. But listen, you sure you don't want to come on out? We can get T-shirts printed up that say 'I rode the wave.'"

"You're nuts." Wes shook his head. He hardly remembered when the last ice meteor from the outer system had been pushed here. He and Jaimee had been only six or seven at the time.

"Maybe. But I'm not going to be sitting on the sidelines when this one hits."

Wes gave up and watched the Jet Ski out on the shallow lake, turning circles around a little island they had explored dozens of times. True, ice asteroid collisions on Mars didn't happen every day. And though no one had expected this one, it promised a big, bad splash.

Still, Wes would much rather watch from the safety of shore than from out there. Jaimee *was* a little nuts, and Wes didn't mind reminding him again. He also reminded him that security would be there any time to clear the big crater lake where the iceberg asteroid would hit and add its life-giving water to the dry Martian atmosphere. They could sure use it.

"Well, they can't catch me if they can't see me. I think I'll just . . ."

Jaimee's voice cut out as he steered his small craft behind the rocky shore of the island, so Wes upped the com's range three ticks, then four. He shouldn't have let Jaimee go out there alone in the first place. But maybe now he could blast some sense into him.

"Come on, Jaimee," he yelled into the com, "don't be stupid. You can't hide out there. And when they find you, you'll be toast."

Ester caught her breath as she stared at the ceiling. And her heart still pounded in her ears at the sound of the strange voice. Sort of like Daddy's holophoto, and Daddy was the only real person she had ever heard speak her language before. Well, and Mommy too, only that was different. Now Ester held her hands over her ears. It was as if God himself had decided he was tired of speaking with the quiet voice of the stars and had decided to repair the radio that had never worked (like half the other systems on the ship).

"Come on," the voice crackled. "You know you can't hide forever."

That burst Ester's idea that she had just imagined the booming voice, and she slowly lifted her hands from her ears. If it *was* God talking, she would need to hear, like Moses's "I Am" or Samuel's voice in the night, just like it said in the Book. Not that she expected God to talk to *her*, but she would be listening, just in case.

For a few minutes, all she heard was a hissing. So she just listened and wondered who would have told her not to be stupid and that she would be in trouble if they found her. And what was she supposed to say back? Speak, for your servant listens?

No. It didn't take long for Ester to decide that God wouldn't be talking to *A-13*, at least not like this. So she had better check outside, the way she was going to do before the jolt, just to be sure the voice had nothing to do with what had scraped the hull. She flipped on the light and peered out the forward view port to see . . .

"Oh!"

The effect made her head spin, as if she had just woke up in a dream of another place—a place that looked like home but wasn't. Stars had never ever shown through the forward view port, only the jagged, unshaven face of Ice. She blinked back the confusion and tried to think. A large chunk must have broken off, exposing part of her ship and a com dish. And straight ahead, a brightening orb made her blink even more.

"Jaimee!" The voice filled her world once again. "I see security coming up the trail, and they've got their lights flashing. You really want to head back now."

Jaimee. That sounded like a name. The com keyboard lit up bright blue, though it never had before, while a digital readout flashed instructions: "Reply, press 1." She'd never actually done this before. But she reached out her hand.

"Jaimee!" came the voice once more. "Are you hearing me? This is serious."

Sirius? That would be the name of the other person, probably named after the star. Before Ester could talk herself out of it, she held down the button marked "1" and leaned close to the com.

"Sirius? Are you Sirius?"

It seemed like a good question.

"There you are. Of course I'm serious. And if you don't get back here right now, you're going to be sorry."

"I . . . I'm not sorry. I'm Ester. This is *A-13*."

Wes adjusted the frequency to make sure he was hearing straight. Either Jaimee was pulling another stunt, or the voice at the other end of the com line wasn't his friend.

"Come again, Jaimee? What are you doing *now*?"

There was a slight pause then, "I said, this is Ester, not . . . Jaimee. I'm from *A-13*. Are you on the planet ahead?"

By this time, Wes was pretty sure his friend couldn't pull off a scam like this, even if he could scramble the signal to make his voice sound so different. Jaimee would be giggling and snorting by this time. But what about *A-13*? What kind of number was that?

"I thought only asteroids had *A* numbers."

"This is an ice asteroid. *A-13*."

"But if you're not Jaimee, and if you *are* really up on that ice pusher, you're headed straight for a crash-down in the middle of Gusev Crater Lake."

The person on the other end didn't say anything for a while. Wes tried again.

"Hello?"

"I'm still here."

"Well, you shouldn't be. Aren't you supposed to bail out or something?"

Ester still wasn't sure how things could have gone so wrong so fast. First Ice had broken apart, and that was bad enough. Now this boy was trying to tell her she was going to crash, and she couldn't believe Daddy would have allowed this to happen. He'd promised the ship would take care of itself. God would take care of her. And she hadn't held on all these years just to crash into some planet, no matter what the boy tried to tell her. If there was any way for her to work the ship's thrusters, change course, now would be the time.

So she tried, but the autopilot wouldn't let go of its grip on *A-13*. The planet up ahead seemed only to grow larger, until it nearly filled the view port the way Ice once had. The boy on the communicator begged her to leave her home world. How could she?

For such a time as this?

She glanced down at the page once more to remind herself what Queen Esther had done in the Book. Queen Esther hadn't lived in a place like *A-13*. But Ester guessed even Queen Esther might have had better luck bringing their frozen thrusters to life.

"Please, Father," Ester prayed as she punched a reset button again and again. "Don't let my home world end."

"She said *what?*" The security scout, a no-smiles guy named Anton with a scruffy beard, still looked as if he was having a hard time with Wes's story. He pushed at a clump of *Deschampsia martiana* (Martian hairgrass) with the toe of his boot.

"She said it was *A-13*, that it was her home and she wasn't going to let it crash. Something about not letting her father down. Then she cut me off."

The young officer shook his head while his face turned red and blue from the rack of lights mounted on the top of his rover.

"If you kids spent as much time in the history database as you did playing around on the lake, you'd know the first twenty ice pushers never made it. And that includes *A-13*. Nobody's had contact with it for sixty years."

"But I'm telling you, she said *A-13!*"

Anton shrugged his shoulders. "I think your buddy's been pulling your leg, 'cause there's nobody on that berg. Autopilot's taking it in, smack into the center of the lake, just like it was supposed to."

At least Jaimee had finally returned to shore. Maybe Wes's threats and the flashing lights had convinced him. Suddenly the officer's expression changed when he touched the com link clamped to his ear.

"What do you *mean*, it's off course?"

Ester gripped the joystick, searching the screen for more clues, another way to power past the planet. Any way. So far, she'd managed only to shut off the autopilot and wake one maneuvering thruster, and that only for a few seconds. Not enough. And now the boy's voice came back at her.

"Ester, I know you can hear me!"

She could hear the desperation in his voice. But what could he tell her that he hadn't said already? She tried another combination of commands and stayed away from the com link. No time for a chat . . .

"Listen, Ester. Your asteroid is headed straight for Delta Colony now. My parents live there. My friends live there. I don't know why you're off course. But if you were on auto-pilot before, put it back on and get out of there. Now!"

By now Ester could taste blood on her lip, and she realized how hard she had been gripping the control handle. *For such a time as this?* There had to be something else she could do to steer clear of this planet. And no, obviously she didn't want to aim her home world into a collision with a colony, but . . .

She just wasn't sure she could turn back on the auto-pilot she'd disabled.

Wes huddled on the ridge of the crater, his back now to the lake, shivering in the cold breeze sweeping in from the southern highlands. It would be the last time he'd see Delta Colony, the red planet's third-largest city, an odd assortment of biodomes and towers clustered on the smooth plains to the north of the crater lake. His home.

And though they'd tried, they couldn't get through to Dad and Mom, not to Jaimee's parents either—"All channels are reserved for emergency workers."

It wouldn't matter. But it would have been nice to say good-bye.

"Two minutes." Anton ticked off the countdown no one wanted to hear. In a matter of seconds, their home would be spectacularly flattened by a giant snowball several miles across, steered there by a crazy space girl who didn't want her world to die. Well now *both* their worlds were doomed.

"Sixty seconds."

They huddled behind an outcropping, waiting for the whistling sound of the icy asteroid, and now he didn't want to hear anything, didn't want to see. He ducked his head between his knees, counting, his tears falling to water the patch of moss below his feet.

Thirty seconds. And in the final moments of her home world, Ester felt strangely calm, almost at peace. Almost. The autopilot had kicked back in. But even with her ship shaking and vibrating, she reached for the Book and her holopicture, just to be sure. The Book was there, but—

"No!" The photo must have drifted away in all the confusion. And now she wouldn't have time to hear her daddy's voice once more before the end. With tears in her eyes, Ester felt a jolt as the dying *A-13* entered the planet's atmosphere.

"I am so sorry . . ." she whispered. "I didn't mean for it to happen like this."

Wes clutched his head between his knees and wanted to scream. Instead, the ice meteorite did it for him, entering the thin Martian atmosphere and hissing toward its target.

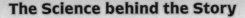

The Science behind the Story

Mars, the Green Planet?

People have been dreaming about visiting Mars for a long time, but we haven't always been sure what's been going on up on the red planet. What happened to all that water that carved those Martian valleys?

Scientists have some pretty good guesses, and most of them have to do with Mars losing its atmosphere, the breathable layer of air that protects a planet from things like the sun's radiation and falling space junk.

What if people could figure out a way to bring the atmosphere back to Mars? If we could melt any water that's still there in the form of ice, the resulting pressure from water vapor could help restore a breathable atmosphere. Plants would add to the atmosphere if scientists could import plants hardy enough to stand the Martian cold. More atmosphere would help the planet slowly warm up. And then . . . Well, the possibilities are mind-boggling. But serious scientists have suggested serious plans. Huge orbiting mirrors could focus sunlight on the Martian polar ice caps to melt them and refill some of the Martian lowlands (like in our story). Another idea is to attach rocket engines to some of the big ice chunks floating around on the edges of the solar system. Though it could take ten to twenty years to wrestle snowballs the size of Connecticut all the way to Mars, it would take only a few such snowballs to add a considerable dose of ice (water) back into Mars's atmosphere.

As we look to the wild possibilities of remolding entire planets, we face yet another question: Just because we can, should we? That's where ethics—doing the right thing—collides with science. Hopefully, when the time comes, some engineers will look to the wisdom of the Bible for answers.

Moments later they felt the earth shudder and heard the awful smack of the giant iceball hitting . . .

Gusev Crater Lake? He fell to his knees, rolled from the jolt, and tumbled into Jaimee's side.

"Holy slushball!" Wes hollered over the roar of water, kilometers behind them. "It splashed!"

And now, after the first shock, they all knew what that meant. Jaimee laughed and stared back at the mushroom cloud of mist and water where the asteroid had made its bull's-eye belly flop into the huge lake. Even the security guard raised his hands to the stinging mist and joined their laugh.

But Wes couldn't laugh when he remembered the thin voice, the girl who had ridden her ice world to its end here. Ester. Her name was Ester. And he couldn't force back a smile with that thought still caught sideways in his mind. It was enough to make him choke on how wrong it was.

Ester gripped the Book; now it was all she had left. She might gladly have traded the slim escape pod for the photo, which had been lost, leaving her with the aching disappointment of knowing she had let her father down. Why had she believed the boy and returned *A-13* to its first path? For the first time since Ice had fallen away, she had time to cry.

And yet . . . the Book still said what it said. That much she knew. So she held her finger on the Verse as she felt the odd swaying motion of the pod hanging by its parachute, drifting slowly to the surface of the planet that had destroyed her home world.

And who knew? Maybe she really *was* put in this place for such a time as this.

Talismort led us out of the hub. "I know what you would like to see," he said gleefully. "This way."

The ship was making another one of its strange sounds as we followed our odd host down a curving corridor. The pearl lights pursued Talismort as he walked. Or did they flick on ahead of him? Did the ship know something?

The sound grew louder until it seemed to be coming through the wall just beside Talismort. He stopped, leaned over, and cocked his ear toward the bulkhead. He gave a little nod and slammed his fist against the wall. The sound stopped.

As he continued down the walkway, he said, "One must know how to fix things in deep space, yes?"

He led us into a circular room with huge glass windows. A cushioned seat ringed the room like a theater. In the center of the chamber was a long tube that stretched from floor to ceiling. Glowing lights danced inside it.

Through the windows we could see vast metallic panels glistening in the feeble sunlight. One of them had a long crack in it, and at the end of the crack were scorch marks.

Talismort swept his hand before him. "This is one of my observation decks." He nodded toward the window.

"If you like stories, there's one behind those injuries to my poor space station."

"Looks like you had some trouble recently," I said, using my I'm-practically-an-adult-now voice.

"More like four hundred years ago. That's when it all started, anyway. Back on Earth. They called it the golden age of piracy. It was a time of majestic ships plowing through the green waters of the Caribbean, of cool sea breezes whistling through rigging before the thunder of cannon fire tore the air. There were great sea battles waged by men with daggers in their mouths and flintlocks in their hands."

Amy put her hand up to her mouth like some dramatic soap opera actress. "You were attacked by pirates?"

Talismort fixed his eyes on us.

"You see, piracy is simple greed. The gold doubloon too often held more charm than the safe shipment of honest goods. So they made their way across the deep waters: black voids with only a thin sheet of clear blue separating the sailors from the darkness below." He looked back through the window and became very serious.

"And it's still the same today. New ships plow through a new ocean, darker and deeper than the first. The distances between the planets are great and difficult to patrol. The time is again ripe for piracy. This time, it's the ocean of interplanetary space. And there are new pirates. The one I ran into had quite a colorful history. They called him Redbeard."

Planetary Pirates

Michael Carroll

Yoshi and Emma bounded
through the airlock like two
gazelles in blue pressure
suits. They bounced more
than walked in the low gravity of Ganymede. Emma glanced
down at the gunpowder-colored dirt,
then looked up. There was no getting around it: the rock-
and-ice landscape of Jupiter's biggest moon was boring.
Gray dust, gray craters with shadows as black as the sky,
gray boulders and pebbles. Gray, gray, gray, with just a
few stripes of blue or tan staining the crater walls. It was
enough to make a girl crazy, and for an artist it was even
worse. There were canyons to the west, and they were
cool. Three canyons wandered next to each other, and
each made Earth's Grand Canyon look like a gravel pit.

She liked painting there, but it was such a long rover drive that she couldn't go often.

Beyond Ganymede's dead horizon, it was another story. The swollen globe of Jupiter loomed above the distant hills. Canyons and mountains of clouds stretched across the planet's face, making brown and white and orange curls and waves. Storms the size of Earth wheeled across the foggy blue-gray south, and to the left, where things were in twilight on Jupiter, Emma could see lightning bolts crackling in the deep cloud valleys. One day, humans would set up floating cities in those clouds and stroll along balconies, watching the sun set in Jupiter's colorful sky. That, Emma thought, would be a good day. Yoshi wasn't so sure. He said he liked Jupiter at arm's length. He called it "that big, scary basketball in the sky."

Their home away from home was the spaceport at Phrygia, a bright rift valley on the Jupiter-facing side of Ganymede. All of Jupiter's big moons kept the same face toward Jupiter, just like the same side of the moon always faced Earth. Jupiter didn't rise or set but stayed in the same place in the sky day in and day out.

"What's that thing?" Yoshi's voice crackled in Emma's headset. He pointed into the sky toward a flashing object.

"Ship," Emma said. "Big one." She squinted, wishing she could scratch her head through her helmet. "It looks funny though. Like it's spinning."

The ship flashed against the black sky, coasting toward the landing tunnel at the edge of Phrygia Spaceport. Closer and closer it came, looking like some immense, crippled whale. Fins and silver skin hung from tangled masses of metal and dangling cable.

"What happened to them?" Yoshi said.

"Some kind of explosion, maybe?"

"Hey, wait a minute. That's not just any ship. That's the police frigate!"

"It's huge!" Emma said.

"Dad told me it was in port at Ganymede while they're watching for pirates around the Jupiter neighborhood."

"He ought to know," Emma said.

Yoshi's father was head of security for the Galilean satellites, the four big moons of Jupiter. He knew lots of cool stuff, like what famous people were arriving and when the next shipment of vid disks was due.

The craft lurched dangerously as vapors erupted from its torn side. Slowly, carefully, the great ship stabilized as its crew struggled to fly it safely into the round opening in the ground. It was only a hundred feet above the tunnel entrance when something went horribly wrong. The right wing dipped, and the entire cruiser twirled around. It spun out of control like a leaf in a wild whirlwind, then slammed into the icy surface. A slurry of ice and gravel sloshed into the air, then drifted to the ground in slow motion. The huge ship settled in a cloud of snow. The hint of a rainbow scattered through the floating ice crystals. Yoshi and Emma were already headed back through the spaceport door.

"Let's find out what happened!" Emma hollered into her helmet microphone.

They bounced down the corridor toward the landing platform. Through the window, they could see an emergency team attaching a flexible tunnel to the side of the craft. The technicians sealed it against the frigate door. As soon as the tunnel was filled with air, the medical unit dashed through it, with Emma and Yoshi close behind. The medical officer at the front of the group banged on the hatch. The door flew open. The ship's captain fell out against one of the medics. He said only one word:

"Pirates."

"Yoshi, you know better," Mr. Namaguchi was saying. "And so do you, young lady. The two of you had no business in that corridor."

"Sorry, Dad."

Emma looked at the floor. "Me too. Sorry."

"Emma, I'm supposed to be keeping an eye on you while your parents are on Europa, and it doesn't make me, the head of security, look too good when you guys run off and pull a stunt like that. The med team doesn't need any teenage supervision in a crisis."

Emma could tell that Mr. Namaguchi was fuming, but Yoshi pushed on. "But, Dad, I still don't get it. Why would pirates attack them this close to Jupiter and then just run away?"

Emma jabbed Yoshi in the ribs. "You just don't know when to stop, do you?"

Mr. Namaguchi grinned and wagged his thumb at Emma. "She knows you well, Yosh! Look, kids, I want you to know what's going on before the rumors start to fly. You guys know how famous Redbeard is."

"Yeah," Yoshi piped up, "I saw him on the cover of the *NewsNow* vid last month."

"That's right, and part of his fame lies in his ship. The *Revenge* is the fastest ship in the solar system. It can go anywhere, and it can outrun anybody else. Our short-range police ships can't catch it."

Emma leaned forward. "Yeah, but what about the long-range ships?"

"Redbeard times his arrivals so that our long-range ships are in other places. It takes a long time to get to Jupiter from somewhere like Mars or the asteroid belt, where a lot of the piracy is taking place."

Yoshi pointed toward the window. Outside, the police ship was being repaired near the edge of the landing tunnel. He turned back to his father. "So while you're chasing pirates out in the asteroids, Redbeard is busy supplying his ship where he can't be caught."

Mr. Namaguchi held up his hand. "So far. But if we could only get to him with one of our long-range cruisers . . . Problem is, he's in and out too quickly. And now the only frigate stationed at Jupiter is disabled. Can you figure out what that means?"

Emma jumped in. "Redbeard is probably on his way here."

"And we can't possibly get the frigate fixed in time to catch him. That ship of his is the brain center for the pirates throughout the solar system. If only we could get him."

"Why don't you just arrest him when he gets here?" Yoshi said.

"Without that frigate, we have no armed ships. It would be like trying to arrest an army."

Emma frowned. "Seems like all you would need is a few minutes with the ship's computer and you could pretty much shut down the whole operation."

Mr. Namaguchi nodded. "Yep, but our spies can't get past his guards. His ship can outgun and outrun all of our local space cruisers. And with the crash of the police frigate, we have no protection, except officers here on the ground."

Emma gazed out the window at the starry sky. "So Redbeard's on his way here, and nobody can do anything to stop him."

"That's the gist of it. So I want you kids to stay inside

for the next few days. There's no telling when or where these pirates will show up."

Yoshi shrugged at his dad, then turned to wink at Emma. He was definitely up to something.

Ever since Mr. Namaguchi's little lecture, it seemed that everybody had something important to do. Everybody, that is, except Emma. The engineers were shoring up domes and windows in case there was some kind of attack. The people at the spaceport tower were monitoring the space chatter to see if there were any clues about where the *Revenge* might be lurking and when it might arrive. The police were doing policey things, as was Mr. Namaguchi. Everyone had a purpose. Everyone had a talent that could be put to use in the crisis. Everyone except her.

"I'm stuck here on this iceball for another three weeks," she mumbled, leaning her forehead against the glass. The observation deck was her favorite place to pout.

"Hey, Emma, c'mon! Let's go outside!"

Emma turned in time to see Yoshi slam into her.

"Whoa! I still haven't learned to stop in time. Sorry, kiddo. You okay?"

Emma gave him a gentle shove, which sent him bouncing off the ceiling. "Fine," she said flatly.

"Ah, you need some cheering up! Do you know how high you can jump here?"

"Well, let's see. I can jump about two feet high on Earth, about six feet on Mars, so here it should be about . . . twelve feet. I could jump over *you*."

Yoshi put his hand on Emma's shoulder. "C'mon, Em. Do you good to get out."

The Science behind the Story

The Mega Moons of Jupiter

The giant planet Jupiter is so big, you could fit a thousand Earths inside it. And talk about moons! Scientists have counted more than sixty! Many of these moons are no larger than big mountains, but four of them are really big. And each moon is unlike any moon or planet anywhere else in our solar system.

Take Callisto. It's the farthest of the biggies from Jupiter and is nearly as big as Ganymede. It's covered with craters like the earth's moon. Callisto's face is covered in brown dust, but ice mountains and cliffs stick out of the dust here and there. Callisto's surface is mostly frozen water, but it has a rock core.

Next in is our friend Ganymede, the king of moons—it's bigger than the planet Mercury! Like Callisto, it's an ice world, but its rocky core is larger. Ganymede may have a deep ocean of slush under its frozen, mountainous surface. Ganymede has wandering canyons that look like they were carved by a giant's fork. Ganymede would make an ideal outpost for humans. Deadly radiation streams from Jupiter, but Ganymede is far enough away that we could set up cities like Phrygia Spaceport.

Europa is a big ball of ice. But it's what's under the ice that has people excited—a deep ocean. This ocean may have volcanoes on a rocky ocean floor. Some people even think there might be living things swimming around down there. The water under Europa's surface causes its ice shell to crack into beautiful ridges and valleys.

Io, Jupiter's fourth big moon, is the closest of the big four to Jupiter. It's called the pizza moon, because it looks like a cheese and pepperoni pizza. Its bright colors come from powerful volcanoes all over it. Some of these volcanoes shoot three hundred miles into the sky.

"I still need to do five more paintings for my class. And I'm tired of painting that!" She shoved her finger toward the desolation outside. She frowned.

Yoshi was smiling. "I bet that's not the real reason. Come on." He yanked on her hand, pulling her toward the hatch.

"Whatever happened to staying inside? Your dad would have your hide."

"Dad just sent some techs outside, and he said I could go if I stayed close."

Emma stood up, hit her head on the ceiling, and reached for her pressure suit.

Outside, the wrecked ship had been moved. The landing tunnel was open for business, sitting like a black mouth on a rumply gray hillside. Rows of landing lights on the tunnel walls made lines that led to the landing pad at the bottom. Somewhere down there stretched a web of underground passages that made up most of Ganymede's Phrygia Spaceport. The landscape next to the tunnel port was clean. There was no sign of the crashed frigate. The spaceport was ready for interplanetary ships again, just waiting for Redbeard's *Revenge* to touch down.

Yoshi led Emma out into the frozen wilderness. They jumped high into the airless sky, then bounced when they came down. Two moons were up: the cold white orb of Europa, hanging low in the sky, and closer to Jupiter, the bright red glowing crescent of Io, the volcanic moon. They made their way to the tunnel. Emma got on her hands and knees and peered down into its darkness. At the bottom she could just make out the soft light of the control rooms and airlocks where the ships docked.

"Last one to the mountain's a black hole." Yoshi called in Emma's headset. She sat up. He was already halfway to the pile of rocks they called "the mountain." She didn't move.

"C'mon, chicken!"

She still didn't move.

Yoshi came back. He sat down beside her, which isn't easy to do when your butt wants to float. "Okay, what's up? You've been depressed for a week."

Emma glanced toward the main domes of the spaceport. People were going from place to place, doing all kinds of important things. "Look in there, Yoshi. All those people have a task. They all have some talent God has given them, and they're using their talents to get ready for the pirates or to fix things. I know God doesn't waste anyone. Everybody has *some* gift. But right now, I can't think of what mine is."

Yoshi slapped his knee. It wasn't a good idea. He began a slow backward somersault. As he tumbled, he scolded her.

"You're the best artist I know. The student league wouldn't have sent you all this way if it wasn't true. Your paintings are beautiful, and they'll show people on Earth what life is like out here."

Yoshi rolled to a stop.

"Maybe so, but what am I going to do, paint a big sign that says 'No Pirates'?"

"I don't think that would work."

Emma stood carefully. "Let's get back. That tech team is headed for the airlock."

Once inside, they took their helmets off. There was a strange hush over the station, a feeling of excitement. Or fear. On their way down the corridor, the kids stopped outside the security office. They could hear raised voices. Yoshi cracked the door just enough to listen. Mr. Namaguchi was speaking to a police officer.

"You heard the guy. They're going to help themselves. Waltz right into Phrygia Spaceport and take what they please. I'm worried for our people."

"If the rumors are true, we don't stand a chance against them. How can you capture fifty armed men? We have small sidearms. That's it."

"Let's face it. Phrygia Spaceport is a cosmic sitting duck."

Yoshi grimaced and closed the door. "Let's get outta here."

Back in Emma's room, Yoshi paced, mostly a few inches above the floor. "If only there were a way to get the pirates off their ship without their weapons. Get them off in a hurry. Then Dad and the police could lock these pirates up once and for all."

Emma was silent. She was doodling on a compupad.

"Em, this is no time to be drawing. What are we going to do?"

She looked up at him, a curious smile across her face. "I think I know. We need some large tarps or sheets of material, maybe foil. And black paint. Lots of it. I just figured out a way to use my gift."

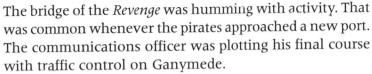

The bridge of the *Revenge* was humming with activity. That was common whenever the pirates approached a new port. The communications officer was plotting his final course with traffic control on Ganymede.

"We're coming in at thirty point zero seven," the officer said into his headset.

"We copy, *Revenge*. Please enter the number two docking port."

"Two? Number two?" Redbeard's voice boomed over

the general bedlam. "Well, well. They finally built another docking bay; how nice." He grinned a picket fence smile.

"Come in at a speed of ten meters per second," the radio crackled.

Redbeard stormed across the weightless room, two feet off the floor; he was fond of making scenes at critical times. He grabbed a headset and turned it on.

"What d'ya mean, ten meters per second?" he demanded. "Isn't that a bit fast?"

There was a pause, then the voice said, "It's standard for the low Ganymede gravity."

Redbeard turned to his pilot. "All right, Skully. We don't want no trouble here. We'll do it their way . . . for now."

"Aye, sir."

The immense ship would fit easily into the dock. The pilot could see the closed port and the second port next to it, open and dark, like a gaping hole. The ship approached quickly, per the instructions from Phrygia Spaceport control. It wasn't until the last few seconds that the crew saw the difference between port two and the other doorway. Port two wasn't a dark tunnel at all. And the lights on its walls were *painted* on!

Emma and Yoshi stood side by side on the observation deck, watching the pirate ship descend toward what appeared to be a docking tunnel. As the nose of the ship struck the painted black surface, the evil vessel collapsed. Officials ran out to "welcome" the pirates with their guns drawn.

A cheer went up in the control room. Several people

shook Emma's hand. The spaceport took on a party atmo-sphere. Outside lay the scarred remains of the largest and most convincing painting Emma had ever done, a painting of a tunnel with rows of lights.

Yoshi slapped Emma on her back as the police and the med team brought the pirates in through the airlock. The buccaneers were wheezing and coughing. Some had to be carried on grav stretchers. But the main part of them that was injured was their pride. They had fallen for Emma's trap in a big way.

Yoshi gave Emma a high five. "That was one great masterpiece."

"Biggest painting I ever did. God never lets our gifts go to waste." Emma looked outside at the shipwreck. "Wow, look how the sun sparkles on the solar panels. I gotta paint that!"

The panels outside shimmered in the sunlight, displaying the blackened burn marks of past pirate attacks. We could see most of the ship from the observation deck. It was an impressive vessel, with turrets and spires, antennas and engine pods. But what held my attention now was the column in the center of the room; it was throbbing with energy.

Talismort followed my gaze. I must have been staring. Bad habit of mine.

After a few quiet moments, he spoke. "It's a conduit to the mainframe computer of the ship. A sort of highway for cyber thoughts. The computer's main artery, linking it to the rest of the ship."

"Is it powerful, your computer?" I asked.

"Is Mount Everest high? Is Pluto cold? Is Valles Marineris deep? You have no idea!" As he said the words, he waved his arms. The movement popped him completely off the floor. "Whoa! You must excuse me," he said as he settled back to the ground. "This room is close to the center of the station, so gravity here is very low. I'm sure you felt it as you came in. Or didn't feel it, as the case may be. It's less than the gravity of the earth's moon here."

"Feels nice," Amy said.

"Yes, but one must be careful. When you live in lower gravity, you must operate differently. Everything is different. Walking, working, even playing. I remember the pole vaulter in the 2206 Mars Olympics who almost sent himself into orbit. He wasn't used to the low gravity. Or that fellow on the moon. What was his name? Ian something . . ."

The Right Path

Marianne Dyson

In the low lunar gravity, the knife spun slowly in the air and struck the gym floor with a clatter. Even before the knife came to rest, Sarah had laid down her staff and started doing pushups.

"*Hah Nah, Dul, Set, Net*," Sarah and the other students counted out loud in Korean. In the Korean martial art of *Kuk Sool*, whenever a higher rank dropped a weapon, all lower ranks stopped and did pushups with them. Losing control of a weapon showed that the student required more practice and discipline—and if a higher ranked student required it, then obviously the lower ranks did too.

As Sarah finished, the new black belt from Earth who had lost the knife passed in front of her, wiping the weapon on his sweat-soaked uniform. "Stupid lunar knife!" He looked at Sarah and said, "I hope you like pushups, because this knife is about as slippery as a fish!" He stumbled back to his practice area.

"Yes, sir. I need more practice, sir!" Sarah responded as respect demanded.

Sarah actually liked doing pushups. They kept her bones and muscles strong so she could compete in Kuk Sool tournaments while she lived on Earth with her mother each summer. During the school year, she lived with her father here in Aristarchus City.

Tomorrow the Kuk Sool grand master himself would be here on the moon. He would oversee black belt testing and watch public demonstrations the students had prepared.

Sarah resumed practicing the staff routine she'd planned for tomorrow. She was a *Dahn Boh Nim*, a brown-black belt. She would earn her fifth black stripe tomorrow. She needed at least three more to qualify for black belt, which she hoped to do before her fifteenth birthday next fall. Maybe then her father would realize Kuk Sool was more than just "an excuse to go exercise with boys."

Sarah had liked being on the girls' volleyball team in middle school, but it hadn't challenged her like Kuk Sool. In Kuk Sool, she competed only with herself. No one accused her of showing off when she did her best. Instead, they encouraged her to try even more difficult techniques. There was always more to learn.

Her father didn't understand. He said if she wanted to learn that "useless" self-defense stuff, she could pay for it herself. Fortunately, God had provided an opportunity for her. Her pastor had introduced her to some uranium miners who gladly paid her to do their laundry. She'd saved the money for months and finally had enough to buy her own staff in time for the big event.

She expertly twirled the five-foot ceramic staff. On

Earth, staffs were made of wood. But wood had to be imported to the moon, so it was as expensive as gold on Earth. Lunar staffs came in different colors. Sarah chose blue for the skies of Earth. She lay on her back and spun the staff above her, watching the light move up and down the shaft. Around and around and— *Thwack!*

"Yow!"

Sarah immediately realized what had happened. The black belt had thrown the knife and, not being used to the lunar gravity, had missed the target completely. It had hit her staff and ricocheted back at him. The knife had chipped the staff and cracked it! She felt sick. She didn't have money for a new one. She'd have to brace it with duct tape. It would be ugly but serviceable. She left her staff and hopped over to the black belt.

"Sir, are you okay?" Sarah asked the young man. She guessed he was a recent high school grad come to the moon on foreign exchange before college.

He glared at her in anger while rubbing his thigh. "You idiot! Your staff got in the way of my knife and threw it back at me!"

Sarah bit her lip. He had called her an idiot and blamed the accident on her. Yet he was a higher rank, and it wouldn't be right for her to challenge him.

Before she could think of something to say, he said, "You shouldn't have been practicing so close!"

"Sir, that may be true, but do you realize you need six times more room for throwing on the moon than on Earth?"

He scowled at her. "Of course I know that."

Sarah had a feeling he knew it in his head but not in practice. Still, no good would come of criticizing a higher rank. She knelt and bowed. "I am sorry, *Jo Kyo Nim*," she said, calling him by his title. "I was not paying attention."

"Well, don't let that happen again!" he growled over the counting of the other students doing pushups.

"Yes, sir," Sarah said, and she meant it. She would pay close attention to this clumsy black belt so his ignorance wouldn't harm him or others.

Sarah scanned the growing crowd in the bleachers for her father. Testing was over, and as usual, everyone had passed. But the true test was not how you performed in front of the judges, but how you performed in class every day. *Sort of like being a Christian*, Sarah thought. *After all, God isn't watching only on Sunday.*

"I bet that guy wouldn't last thirty seconds in a sparring match with Master Harmon!" a familiar voice said.

Sarah turned to face and bow to her friend Julie. Julie was new to Kuk Sool, but she was a fast learner and already a blue belt, just two ranks below brown.

"What guy?" Sarah asked.

"That new black belt from Earth," Julie said. She tipped her head toward a guy wearing a silver-trimmed dress black belt uniform. Sarah sighed. One of those outfits would cost her six months of laundry earnings.

"Oh, that guy!" Sarah said, suddenly recognizing him. "He missed the target last night at practice and cracked my staff."

"Your new staff! How awful!" Julie said.

Sarah shrugged. "Thank goodness for duct tape, huh?"

"I guess," Julie said. "Did you know he refused to do the adaptation exercises my mom recommended? He insisted he didn't need them!" Julie giggled. "Can you imagine someone telling *my* mother he knows better what's good for him than she does?"

Sarah had to laugh. Julie's mother was the solar system's expert on adaptation to new environments. If she told the president of the United States to crawl across the floor and moo to speed his adaptation, he would do it without hesitation.

"That explains why he was so clumsy last night. He hasn't retrained his muscles to provide the right amount of force." Sarah sighed. *God, I should have tried to help him instead of focusing on my demo last night.*

"Well," Julie said, "maybe a sprained ankle will teach him to listen to my mother!" They shared a laugh. "Speaking of my mother," Julie said, "she's saving us a seat. When your demo is over, come join us. The way the crowd's growing, I think the only people not here are stuck on Earth!"

Except my father, Sarah thought as Julie bounced away to join her demo team. The place really was packed. She spotted Pastor Craig and waved to him. *At least my heavenly Father is watching.*

Sarah stood at attention in the arena with her staff tucked vertically behind her right shoulder, bare feet together. The audience quieted. She bowed to the grand master and said "Kuk Sool" loudly. "My name is Sarah Thomson, and I'll be performing *Ki-bon Bong* adapted for the moon. With your permission, may I begin?"

The grand master nodded his approval. Master Harmon offered a smile of encouragement. Sarah was really lucky to have Master Harmon, the women's world champion in bong techniques, for her instructor.

"Thank you," Sarah said. She bowed again.

She moved smoothly through fifteen standing techniques and then began what was called the moving plum figure-eight spin. Taking advantage of the low gravity, instead of turning in a circle, she jumped into the air and did the entire technique without her feet touching the floor. The audience cheered. Sarah didn't spare any thought for them. She focused on her distance from the floor, pointing her toes, keeping the staff at the proper angle. She became a flower dancing with a whirlwind, beautiful and strong at the same time.

Sarah sailed through the techniques, seeing the sequence of movements as a path in the air that she must trace. Pastor Craig, who was also a pilot, said she was a natural navigator. She just saw how things should move, and her body followed her mind.

She completed the set. The audience went wild with clapping and hooting. Had she been that good, or were they just easily entertained? She hoped she at least had set a good example for the newer students. Anything beyond that was merely proof of Master Harmon's teaching skill.

Sarah bowed and backed out of the ring. She turned to find the new black belt waiting to go on next. She bowed, while he quickly jerked his head. He seemed nervous, or maybe it was just the usual flushed look of newcomers. Sarah was surprised to see him holding a black ceramic staff.

"Are you going to do a bong demonstration, Jo Kyo Nim?" Sarah asked.

"No, I just carry a staff around to feel important," he said sarcastically. "If you're done with your cheerleader routine, it must be time for the real thing. Excuse me." He pushed his way past her into the arena.

Sarah wondered if his rudeness was because he found her attractive. That was one of Julie's favorite theories. She

The Science behind the Story

Lunar Gravity—
the 17 Percent Solution

Lunar gravity is one-sixth that of Earth's gravity. That means that on the moon, objects and people weigh six times less and fall with six times less force. When people go from Earth's gravity to lower gravity, blood shifts to the upper body. (This is because the heart is used to pumping "uphill" against Earth's gravity, and the blood vessels are designed to prevent that blood from "falling" back down too quickly.) People feel as if they're standing on their heads. Their faces get puffy and red, and their noses feel stuffy even though they don't have a cold. The brain senses the changes and "orders" the body to get rid of the excess fluid. One way it does this is by sweating. Most of these changes happen in the first few weeks in space. Eventually, the heart actually shrinks in size because it doesn't have to push as much blood as hard as it does on Earth.

Another change takes place in the inner ears. Fluid pressing against tiny hairs informs the brain what direction the body is moving. After spinning around on Earth, the fluid quickly settles, but not so in space or on the moon. When gravity is reduced, the fluid doesn't press as hard, confusing the person's sense of balance. After a week or so in space, people have "reprogrammed" their brains to interpret movements in their new environment. Doctors have devised exercises for astronauts to use their eyes instead of their ears to determine their orientation and thus speed their adjustment to the new environment.

Kuk Sool is a real Korean martial art, though how its practice will be adjusted on the moon is fictionalized. More information is available at www.kuksoolwon.com. The author is a student of Kuk Sool.

said guys feared being rejected by pretty girls, so they set themselves up to get it over with quickly by being obnoxious. If that was his plan, Sarah thought it was working pretty well.

A junior red belt about ten years old ran up and bowed to Sarah. She held out a copy of the program and a pen. "Dahn Boh Nim, would you sign my program?"

"Me?" Sarah asked. "I'm not even a black belt."

"But you will be soon," the girl insisted. "That demo was awesome!"

"Thank you," Sarah said shyly. She signed the program and then knelt down with the girl to watch the demonstration.

His name was Ian. He announced that he was going to do *Bong Hyung*, staff forms. Forms demonstrated the student's ability to memorize a chain of complex movements, execute them precisely, and do them so smoothly that each motion naturally flowed from the last.

His initial movements were similar to Sarah's demonstration—spinning the staff and striking imaginary targets. He obviously knew the sequence well. Sarah enjoyed the way the flaps of his dress uniform made a ring like Saturn's as he spun. But he leaned to one side whenever he stopped. He was using more power than needed and losing his balance, a common mistake of newcomers to the moon. A few weeks with Master Harmon would break him of that.

The hyung was long though, and it didn't look like Ian was up to it. Most likely, his heart was in overdrive, still acting to overcome Earth's gravity and sending too much blood to his head. His brain would automatically raise his temperature to cause him to sweat away the "excess" fluid. So his face was puffy red, and sweat stains darkened his uniform.

Whack! Ian's sweaty grip slipped and the staff slammed

against the hard floor. If this were a tournament, he would stop after such a bad mistake, and all the lower ranks would do pushups. But this was a demonstration, so he continued.

Sarah saw that the slam had cracked the black staff. She thought of her staff, its beauty marred with duct tape. It seemed appropriate that his would now have to be taped as well. Maybe he wouldn't be as smug after this.

However, it seemed that the mistake had made Ian angry. His knuckles were white against the black staff, and his face was nearly purple. Proper hyung required a clear mind. If he didn't calm down, his concentration would slip as well as his grip. Sarah knew this hyung included a difficult jump spin combination near the end. He was still using too much power in his mock strikes. If he lost his balance . . .

"No!" Sarah said as the staff hurled from Ian's hands toward the crowded viewing stands. Could she stop this potentially deadly spear? She suddenly saw a path in her head. She could do it!

"Catch my staff," she ordered the girl beside her. Then, in a flash of movement, Sarah used her staff to pole-vault sixty feet into the air.

Her aim was true, and she nabbed Ian's staff. She began falling toward the viewing stands. She needed to do another pole vault in the stands to get clear of the crowd. But the people were packed in so tightly, where could she come down? *God, please clear me a spot! Don't let me hurt anyone!*

The fall took six times longer on the moon than it would have taken on Earth. As Sarah dove, she recognized the faces of the uranium miners whose laundry she'd cleaned. And there, in the midst of them, was Pastor Craig! "Clear me a spot!" she yelled.

He slid off his seat and crouched down, covering his head. She aimed the black staff at his empty seat. Now she could pole-vault right over the bleachers and come down on the other side. *Thank you, God!*

The staff made a loud *twang* as it hit the aluminum bleachers. Sarah flipped to the side and glided over the crowd. Soon she was over the top of the bleachers and diving to the floor behind them. It was a thirty-foot drop. Luckily, that was equal to about a five-foot drop on Earth. Still, it was a hard floor. She needed to use the staff to absorb some of her energy.

Sarah held the staff tightly against her right side. The staff hit the floor first and slid a little, slowing her down. But the impact split the staff, and it shattered! Sarah didn't have time to let go before the sharp edges slit her hand. She fell among the pieces, rolling as she'd been trained, her head never touching the floor. Her forearms slapped the surface, and she let out her breath in a loud yell, surprising people in line at the drink stand.

Sarah sat up slowly as a crowd gathered. A voice of authority told them to make way, and Master Harmon knelt beside her. "How are you, Dahn Bo Nim?" she asked.

Sensing nothing broken, Sarah answered, "I'm fine, ma'am."

An emergency medic pulled back Sarah's torn sleeves. The skin of both forearms was scraped raw and bleeding, and her right hand was cut pretty badly.

"Good *nak bub*," Master Harmon said with a smile.

"Yes, ma'am," Sarah said. *Nak bub* was Korean for falling. She was supposed to take the brunt of the fall on her forearms and hands, and she had.

The medic treated Sarah's injuries with spray "skin" made from moon-grown aloe vera. He wrapped her right palm with white bandages, and Master Harmon helped her to her feet.

Her father rushed over to her. "Sarah! Are you hurt? I was on my way here when I got an emergency page from Pastor Craig."

Sarah stared down at her bandaged hand and then into her father's worried eyes. "I'm all right," she assured him. "I know how to fall. I only scraped my arms a little."

Master Harmon nodded. "Your daughter is an excellent student. You must be very proud of her. Her quick action may have saved someone's life today. If you will allow me to take her back to the arena for a few moments, I'm sure the grand master would like to personally thank her."

"Can I go, Father? Please?"

Maybe it was the expression on her face, or maybe it was just that her father saw that arguing with her was useless, but he nodded. Sarah hugged him quickly and thanked him for coming. He said something about getting the time wrong, but Sarah could only be glad that he had come at all.

As Master Harmon escorted Sarah back toward the arena, her father following, Julie dashed over. "You were amazing!" Julie said. "I didn't know you were a pole-vaulter!"

Sarah laughed. "I'm not. It was just the quickest way to get high enough to catch the staff."

"I keep telling her to go out for track," her father said. "I don't understand why she wants to learn self-defense. It's not like we have any muggers on the moon!"

"It is pretty safe here," Master Harmon agreed. "But Kuk Sool isn't just about fighting. It's about body conditioning and mental development as well."

"That's for sure!" Julie added. "My mom says it's the best exercise program on the moon, and that's high praise coming from her. She also likes the idea that I'll be able to protect myself from pushy guys when I go back to Earth."

Sarah knew Julie was talking about Ian, and she smiled.

"That's a good point," Sarah's father said thoughtfully. Sarah guessed he was thinking about her next trip to Earth.

The conversation ended as they reached the participants' area. Sarah's father went to sit with Julie and her mom, while Master Harmon took Sarah into the arena. The crowd erupted in applause. Sarah walked in a sort of daze to the grand master. Ian stood beside him, studying his feet.

They stopped in front of the grand master and bowed. It was quiet now except for the hum of cameras. "Dahn Boh Nim, recite student creed number three," he said.

"Yes, sir," Sarah stammered at this unexpected request. "I will use what I learn in class constructively and defensively to help myself and others and never be abusive or offensive, sir."

"That's right," he said. "When you went after that staff, you acted defensively to help others. Earlier, in your testing and in your demonstration, you showed great strength of body and mind. Therefore," the grand master declared, "on behalf of the World Kuk Sool Association, I hereby certify that you, Sarah Thomson, have met all the requirements for promotion to the rank of first-degree black belt."

Sarah gasped. She had never heard of anyone being promoted to black belt with so few stripes. Yet there stood the grand master himself holding a new black belt just for her. He cleared his throat. "Please raise your arms."

"Yes, sir," Sarah squeaked.

Master Harmon untied her brown belt and folded it. Then the grand master tied the black belt tightly around her waist.

He reached for Sarah's hands and gently held them, careful not to press on the bandages. "Congratulations, Jo Kyo Nim," he said, bowing to her.

She bowed and managed to choke out, "Thank you, sir," around the lump in her throat.

"Now, Jo Kyo Nim, Ian has something to say," the grand master said.

Ian knelt in front of Sarah. "I take full responsibility for the damage caused to your staff during practice last night," he said. "Please allow me to replace it with a new one."

Sarah glanced over at the junior red belt holding her blue staff in the participant's area. The duct tape had held just fine. She didn't really need a new staff. However, she understood that this was Ian's way of repaying her for causing her injury. "Thank you, sir," Sarah said quietly. She expected him to rise, but he continued kneeling.

"I also offer my apology to you for my actions today," he said.

Sarah noticed the grand master nodding his approval. How many times had they recited the first rule in strong mind training: martial arts etiquette! The vid of today's event would doubtlessly be seen by every Kuk Sool student for months to come. Instead of just being an example of how not to do a demonstration, it would now also be a lesson in accepting responsibility and showing respect. She nodded her acceptance. But he wasn't done. "Please allow me to pay for the black belt uniform you earned today, to thank you for preventing my mistake from hurting others."

Sarah gulped. He was offering to pay for a new staff *and* a black belt uniform? Students only got room and board. He'd need a job to pay for these extra expenses. *Hmm.* He could do the miners' laundry while her hand healed!

"You're very generous," Sarah said.

Ian stood up and backed away, flashing a weak smile at her.

Sarah bowed and also left the arena. Surprisingly, Ian was waiting for her. He bowed and offered his congratulations on her promotion. Sarah returned the bow, wondering if being nice meant he didn't like her after all? She would have to ask Julie later. The junior red belt offered her congratulations too and asked what to do with Sarah's staff.

Sarah glanced at Ian. His staff lay in pieces, and people would be making fun of him for weeks. He had called her an idiot. But he had also apologized and seemed genuinely sorry. Sarah remembered all the times she had failed God and yet been given a chance to start over.

"Jo Kyo Nim, you will need a staff to train with us here," she said. "I would be honored if you would accept this one to use while you are on the moon."

Ian grinned, a true smile this time. Sarah thought he looked rather handsome.

"Thank you, Jo Kyo Nim," he said, using her new title. "You are very generous. I will gladly take the staff to the school for you and make sure the staff is properly cleaned. As soon as your hand is healed, I would be honored if you would teach me how to adjust my Bong Hyung for the moon. Obviously, I need more practice!"

Everyone laughed. Maybe Ian would fit in after all.

Sarah said her good-byes and followed her father toward the door.

"Wait," he said. "Did you want to stay and watch the rest of the demonstrations?"

Sarah stopped. She really wanted to, but she felt a need to be with her father too. "Only if you want to," she said.

He smiled. "I suppose my report on the pyroclastic intrusions in lunar anorthosite can wait while I learn what it means to have a black belt for a daughter."

Sarah nearly glowed as she led her father back into the gym.

"But we weren't talking about gravity, were we?" Talismort said. "You asked about the computer, about that impressive column there."

As if to underscore his words, the tube washed itself in waves of gold and silver light. A loud, low growl pulsed through it like the beating of a giant's heart.

"Yes, the mind of the computer. Our machines are merely a reflection of us, you know. We build computers that mimic our thoughts, and devices that do our labor for us, and machines that carry out tasks our bodies are too weak or fragile to do."

"Some of those machines aren't so great," I said. "Like war machines or—"

"Or things that mess up the environment," Amy added. "Things that belch out smoke or tear up the forests."

"Yeah," I said. (Sometimes I'm brilliant.)

Talismort pressed his fingertips together. His hands formed a long steeple, which he rested against his chin. "Each of these machines has a purpose. Some reflect the good in humankind, and others do not. The real problem comes when we begin to rely on our machines. When we let our computers think for us and allow our machines to do all the work for us. Eventually, our machines no longer serve us. They rule us."

Talismort looked up through the dome at the glistening stars. The Milky Way spread a hundred billion stars over our heads in mists of faint blue, crimson, and bronze. He fixed his eyes on the star clouds as he spoke.

"We must keep our minds free from these things. There are, of course, things that can trap our minds. Things like temptation, laziness, or forgetting to love those around us. Paul spoke of keeping our minds keen and focused so we don't fall into mind traps. 'We take captive every thought,' Paul said. Every thought captive."

"And when we don't?" I asked.

"When we get lazy about our thoughts? When we stop caring? A young man named Jeremy was faced with just such a situation."

Time Coffin

John B. Olson

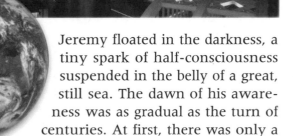

Jeremy floated in the darkness, a tiny spark of half-consciousness suspended in the belly of a great, still sea. The dawn of his awareness was as gradual as the turn of centuries. At first, there was only a flicker. Awareness of nothing except that he hadn't been aware of anything for a long, long time. And then came the sensation of rising, of being slowly, almost imperceptibly drawn upward toward a shimmering light.

The light grew brighter and brighter until his mind was filled with the sound of a great hiss. Cool air rushed to surround him. His burning lungs expanded in a wrenching gasp, his first breath in . . . In how long? He lay on his back, squinting desperately against the light, searching for an answer. It was hours before his tingling body could remember how to respond, hours before he could force his hand away from his face and grope through the light, hours before his sense of touch finally came back, bringing the sensation of cold, smooth metal encasing him like a coffin. And then he remembered. He was in the time machine.

By the time he was able to push the heavy lid off the coffin-shaped box, he had grown strong enough to stand. He scrambled out of the machine and stood leaning against it, squinting against the gloom of a dusty cave. The box lay open before him. Its smooth black surface sucked up the light, making invisible every corner, every seam he had so patiently joined together in a labor of love and obedience. He sat on the coffin's edge, loath to leave his creation for even a moment. It was his only tie to his own world, his only tie to the time where he belonged . . . But he knew he had to go. He had been called into this world for a reason.

Jeremy gave the machine's great lid a farewell pat, then shuffled toward the entrance of the cave, shielding his eyes against the light. He emerged to a dazzling world. It opened up before him like an infinite void. He tottered on the brink of the chasm, steadying himself against a sapling that grew at the world's edge. Everything was so big, so open. Had it always been so . . . terrifying? He clung to the flimsy tree, fighting the urge to run back to the safety of his time coffin. He could do this—would do this.

He stared straight ahead, watching as his surroundings gradually shrank to normal proportions. The world hadn't changed as much as he had feared. At least there were still trees. The tremendous weight of stretched time weighed on him like a wet cloak. If it weren't for that sense, he would have thought he had never left home.

He forced himself to let go of the sapling and stepped

forward in defiance of his terror-stricken senses. The fear would pass in time, a gentle voice in his head assured him. As he staggered forward through the trees, a million subtle differences danced at the edge of his awareness. He was definitely in a different time. He could be mistaken about the piercing nature of the light but not about the dirty, metallic taste of the air he breathed, not about the roars and whines that broke the calm of the woods, not about hundreds of other differences too minute to notice individually but, when taken all together, were as bracing as a slap in the face.

Jeremy pushed through the trees into an open field, and then he saw it. Red and flashing silver, faster than lightning, it sped over a road as smooth as glass. He watched the vehicle less than a second before it disappeared around a distant bend in the road. Such speed! He didn't know whether to be more amazed by the speed of the vehicle or by how easy it was for him to accept it. He had prepared himself for progress, but this had exceeded all expectations.

While he stood staring at the bend in the road, the pounding of heavy footfalls behind him made him spin around. A man ran toward him, a man who, except for his metallic short pants and glowing yellow shirt, might have passed for any other man from Jeremy's time.

"Good day, sir," Jeremy began, as if he were an ambassador addressing a statesman. "My name is Jeremy Jen . . ."

The man ran by without breaking stride, his dull, glazed eyes never even registering Jeremy's existence. A shudder ran down Jeremy's spine. The man's dull face was almost devoid of all humanity. The body was human, but the mind seemed a complete blank. No wonder he had been given the plans; no wonder he had been called to this

The Science behind the Story

Boiling Frogs and Tall Tales

We call it "science fiction," but what does that mean, exactly? They're stories that rely on science to make the plots fun or exciting . . . or just to make us think. They're things we imagine could happen in the future. Or they're stories we know could never happen, but we pretend they could.

Most of the time, sci-fi authors take a bit of real science and project it into the future. Or they take a true scientific discovery and twist it into the shape of a story.

In "Time Coffin," author John Olson takes the familiar time travel idea and turns the clock *back*. We're used to thinking of how weird the world might be two hundred years from now. And we can imagine that if we woke up in a time capsule two centuries from today, we'd be shocked. So wouldn't a time traveler from two hundred years ago be shocked at the bizarre world we live in today?

It's something to think about. And here's one more thing to consider: scientists have shown that there's one sure way to boil a frog. First put him in a pot of cold water, where he's comfortable, and turn the heat on low. Then slowly crank up the heat. The frog doesn't realize what's happening, so after a while he's cooked, but the heat has been building too slowly for him to figure it out.

It's the same way with the world we live in. Olson's character finds out that things are pretty weird in the world he visits, though the people living there don't even realize what's happened. If that's not a scientific principle, it ought to be.

time. But if all the citizens of the United States had been reduced to such a state . . . Jeremy shook his head. What would he be able to do?

While he was still considering the man's sad plight, he looked up and saw a woman approaching at a fast, mechanical walk. Jeremy looked down at the ground in embarrassment and shame. What did she think she was doing, walking around in broad daylight in her underwear? As the woman drew closer and Jeremy grew redder, he became aware of a high-pitched, pulsing whine. Not knowing if the whine was a warning of approaching danger, he looked up long enough to see that it was coming from a strange instrument attached to the woman's head and ears.

He quickly looked back down again, but he had seen enough to confirm his suspicions. The woman was being controlled. Brainwashed. Jeremy's anger and outrage at her lack of modesty slowly gave way to pity. She wore the same blank expression as the man. What kind of a society was this that permitted women to be so exploited? How low must the human race have fallen? The instrument she wore seemed to be designed to keep her from being able to think—to maintain her zombielike state. Surely, she was being controlled against her will. She certainly hadn't volunteered for such treatment. It was too despicable for words. Someone was using the device to subdue her, and that someone was going to have to answer to him!

Jeremy followed her from a discreet distance across an open field, and a new sense of mission burned in his heart. Was he the only man left in this world who could speak forth God's truth to this wicked and perverted generation? Why else would he have been sent?

As he walked, he passed a man sitting on a chair, holding a huge piece of paper. Noting more intelligence and humanity in the man's expression, he hazarded one more attempt at communication.

"Do you understand English?"

"Sure do." The man looked surprised at the question.

"Good. Could I trouble you for the exact date?"

"May 18th."

"And the year?"

"2005."

Jeremy gasped. God had brought him two hundred years into the future just to reach these people. He hoped he hadn't overshot. From the looks of things, it almost seemed too late.

The computer tube pulsed with electric thoughts. As Talismort stood and those little pearl lights followed him around the room, I wondered if the computer was thinking of us. Watching us. Plotting some horrible thing against us. But this place was fun. Talismort was a wonderful host. So why was I so uneasy?

Maybe it was the throbbing sound of that flickering column. I stepped away from it and walked over to the window. I could still hear a faint *thrum . . . thrum . . . thrum . . .* But it wasn't coming from the center of the room. It was coming from beside me. I turned around to see a little plant in a pot on the windowsill. It was no ordinary plant. This one was a startling purple with a crimson fringe on the leaves. The purple stump grew out of a ball-like bulb at the plant's base. Beneath the bulb were piles of what looked like violet spaghetti. Roots? But the really weird thing was that the plant's bulb was making that pulsing sound. In fact, it was beating—like a heart. I thought of scary stories about hearts beating. Edgar Allen Poe stuff. Or really lousy science fiction movies where half the control room is lit with Christmas lights and the monster is a guy dressed up in a rug. This purple pansy was freaking me out.

"How do you like my little garden friend?" Talismort asked. The light from the column washed his face in gold, then red, then blue.

"Kinda creepy," I said. I was thinking as much of Talismort's face as I was the plant.

"Oh yes. A bit bizarre. You should see the world it came from. It's an out-of-the-way place around a distant sun. It was visited once by a starship called *Far Encounter.* The crew found much more than exotic plants there. They found things that changed their lives. Especially a young lady named Kacey."

····················11·····················

Shipwreck Planet

Jim Denney

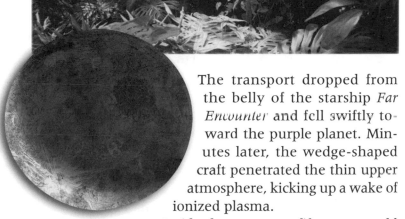

The transport dropped from the belly of the starship *Far Encounter* and fell swiftly toward the purple planet. Minutes later, the wedge-shaped craft penetrated the thin upper atmosphere, kicking up a wake of ionized plasma.

Inside the transport, fifteen-year-old cadet Kacey O'Quinn checked her reflection in the transparent quartz view port. People told Kacey she was pretty, though she didn't think so. She thought her smile was too wide and her chocolate-brown eyes were too big. She thought straight, brown hair was boring, and she despised that sprinkle of freckles across her nose (her friends said they made her look cute, but Kacey *hated* cute).

It was Kacey's fifth planetfall as a Space Fleet cadet—yet she almost didn't get to come. "Too dangerous," her father had said when she requested assignment to the landing party. "A bunch of hijackers crashed a transport on the planet. We may have to shoot it out with photon blasters."

Her fellow cadets told her she was lucky to have a starship captain for a father. Yeah, right! Captain Liam O'Quinn was twice as hard—no, ten times as hard—on Kacey as he was on any other cadet on the ship. Worst of all, he was so overprotective!

After her father had refused to assign her to the landing party, Kacey had said, "Aren't you saying no just because I'm your daughter?"

"That's right," he had said. "I'm saying no because you're my daughter." At that point, Kacey had thought her cause was lost.

Then the captain had added, "And that's not a good reason for saying no. You're right. I've got to treat you like any other cadet in the fleet—so I'm assigning you to the landing party."

So here I am, descending to a new world, she thought as the purple landscape passed by below. *I just hope something exciting happens!*

Kacey was about to get more excitement than she bargained for.

Up in the cockpit, a pair of techbots named Wilbur and Orville sat in the pilot and copilot seats. The lights from the cockpit displays reflected off their polished metal skin. Behind the techbots sat three figures. On the right was Maa Laas, *Far Encounter*'s spiderlike science officer, hunched over the starboard tech display. In the center sat Kacey's father, Captain O'Quinn—a man who truly looked the part of a starship captain, with his keen, gray eyes and his jet-black mustache and hair with just a dash of gray at the temples. On the left sat K'Charr, *Far Encounter*'s four-armed engineer, clad in a protective suit and bubble helmet, leaning over the port-side tech display.

K'Charr was a Krematian, from a world where the surface temperature was roughly five hundred degrees Fahrenheit. Krematians were perfectly suited for the hot, radiation-rich environment of a starship's engine room. Outside the engine room, K'Charr had to wear an oven suit and bubble helmet to maintain his fiery body heat. A transmitter in the helmet enabled him to speak and hear. He had four arms—two massive, powerful upper arms for heavy lifting and two smaller lower arms for precision work. A pair of red-orange eyes glowed from a face that looked like a lump of black coal. When he spoke, wisps of blue flame shot from his mouth.

"Captain," K'Charr said in a deep, rumbling voice, "I have detected the stolen transport. I'm sending locator coordinates to Wilbur's guidance computer."

"Course plotted," Wilbur said in a flat, electronic tone.

Captain O'Quinn asked, "Life scan, Maa Laas?"

Science Officer Maa Laas, of the planet Ankor Edge, resembled a human-size orange spider who walked on four of her eight limbs. Her four upper limbs ended in three-clawed pincers. Her head supported eight eyes that swayed on snaking eyestalks. Her flutelike voice came from a bell-shaped snout beneath her eyes. Like all Ankoreans, Maa Laas had trouble pronouncing the letter *V*.

"Extensif life signs, Captain," Maa Laas said. "Much animal life in forest. Signs of intelligent life detected but no technology, no fehicles, no power generation, no industries. A primitif culture, Captain."

Kacey sat in the troop section, along with a squad of eight troopers armed with photon blasters. From her position just behind the cockpit, Kacey could overhear the cockpit conversation—including the science officer's announcement.

Life! she thought to herself. *Intelligent life! We'll get to meet a whole new race of people! I wonder what they'll look like.*

At an altitude of thirty thousand feet, the craft performed a series of turns to reduce speed. As the transport came out of its final turn, Kacey heard a mechanical whine, indicating that the engine pods were being deployed.

Looking out the view port, Kacey saw a vast purple forest spread out below. From various little clearings in the forest, dozens of smoke plumes rose straight up into the clear, blue-violet sky. Each column of smoke, Kacey realized, must indicate the site of an alien village.

"Wreckage ahead, Captain," Wilbur said. "There's a clearing just east of the wreck. We'll set down close by."

A minute later, the transport passed over a clearing strewn with pieces of white and silver wreckage. Through her view port, Kacey saw the partly crumpled fuselage of a transport that had plowed into the ground. Both of its engine pods were ripped open and blackened, as if they had exploded.

The transport Kacey rode in banked right and came back around. The landing gear extended, and the underside thrusters fired. The vehicle settled lightly to the ground.

Kacey felt a gentle bump. The transport was down.

With a whirring sound, the boarding ramp extended downward from the belly of the vehicle. The team of armed troopers descended first. Next came Captain O'Quinn, Kacey, K'Charr, Maa Laas, and the two techbots.

Maa Laas swayed on her four spidery legs and looked skyward with her eight eyes on waving eyestalks. In several directions, columns of rising smoke were visible over the tops of the purple trees. "Much smoke rises," the science officer observed, "yet atmosphere is clear. Curious."

Captain O'Quinn raised his wrist com and sent a quick status report to the orbiting starship. Then he turned to the squad of troopers. "You four," he said, "stay here and guard the transport. The rest of you—let's check out the wreckage."

The four guards took their positions, and the rest of the landing party crossed the clearing toward the wrecked transport. Kacey walked just behind her father, stepping over twisted bits of metal and blackened chunks of exploded engine.

The captain pointed toward a gaping hole in the midsection of the crashed transport. "Wilbur, Orville, get inside that transport and check out the cockpit. Careful—the hijackers could be inside. K'Charr, check out those engine pods. Troopers, keep your blasters ready. Everybody stay sharp!"

Kacey worried about the two techbots. She knew her father had good reason for sending Wilbur and Orville into the wreckage instead of troopers. If a bot got shot, it could be repaired or replaced. Human beings were hard to repair and couldn't be replaced. She watched tensely as the techbots entered the wreckage—and was relieved when they came back out.

Wilbur and Orville told Captain O'Quinn that the wreckage was deserted. Oddly, the wrecked transport's computer systems were up and running, powered by the solar panels over the cockpit.

"We also noticed," Orville added, "that the ground vegetation around the wreckage is flattened by footsteps. Someone has been inside the wreckage—and very recently."

As the techbot finished its report, K'Charr called the captain over to show him the engine pods. The pods were too mangled and fire blackened to yield many clues. But they did produce one mystery: why did both engines explode at almost the same moment, causing the vehicle to crash?

"Captain!" piped Maa Laas. "You'd better see this." She stood a short distance from the wreckage, at the edge of the purple forest.

Captain O'Quinn and Kacey hurried over to see what Maa Laas had found. They arrived to find the spidery Ankorean science officer standing over four rectangular mounds spaced evenly apart.

Kacey gasped when she realized what the mounds were. "They look like graves!" she said.

"I scanned to depth of two meters," Maa Laas said, gripping her scanner in one set of orange pincers. "Four human bodies buried here."

"Four hijackers stole that transport from the docking bay of the starship *Intrepid*," the captain said. "That was three months ago. Look at the purple grass sprouting on the graves. I don't know how fast grass grows on this planet, but it could be three months' growth. Looks like we found our four hijackers. That only leaves one question: who buried them?"

Kacey felt a thrill of fear. She glanced anxiously around the edges of the clearing. Who were the people of this planet? Were they in the forest, watching at that very moment?

There was a motion among the trees to Kacey's left. She looked—

And screamed!

An inhuman creature stepped out of the shadows of the purple forest. It was eight feet tall, frightening—yet beautiful. The texture and color of the creature's purplish-gray skin reminded Kacey of orchid petals. The head was a bald, chinless dome. The face was featureless, except for a long vertical slit where the nose and mouth should be. Pale gray eyes rose over the top of the head on twin periscope-like eyestalks. The hands ended in clusters of snaky tentacles, and the feet were broad and flat, each with a dozen "toes" that looked like wriggling purplish-gray worms.

The vertical slit in the creature's face fluttered as it spoke. "Welcome to Eréa," the creature said in Kacey's own language. "My name is Urael. The peace of Kyrieh be with you."

Kacey looked from the creature to her father. Captain O'Quinn appeared startled for a moment but quickly recovered. "I am Captain Liam O'Quinn of the starship *Far Encounter*," he said. "This is my daughter, Cadet Kacey O'Quinn. And this is my science officer, Maa Laas. Greetings in the name of the Galactic Community." He started to put out his hand—then halted uncertainly when he saw that Urael's tentacled hand resembled a mass of writhing snakes.

But Urael didn't hesitate to reach out and grasp the captain's hand. The wriggling tentacles of Urael's hand slithered all the way to the captain's elbow. Kacey noticed that her father flinched at the alien's touch.

"How—" the captain began.

"I learned your talking," the Eréan interrupted, "from a machine."

"A machine?" the captain said. "But—"

"I should tell from the beginning," Urael said.

"Please do," the captain said.

Urael pointed a mass of tentacles toward the wreckage. "That flying craft fell out of the sky many days ago." Then he pointed toward a column of smoke that rose above the trees. "I was in my village when I saw the flying craft in the sky. I heard thunder, and I saw a great smoke. I came here with others from my village. We found the flying craft broken. Bodies of men were inside. The spirits were gone from the bodies. We waited to see if the spirits would come back, but they did not. So we put the bodies in the ground. I went into the broken craft, and I found a machine that made light and pictures."

"The computer?" Kacey asked.

"Yes, the computer," Urael said. "I touched the little pictures, and the computer made bigger pictures, talking pictures. For many days, I looked and listened to the machine. I learned your talking—but some words I do not know."

From Urael's description, Kacey could tell that the Eréan had opened the computer's library files. The computer's 3-D touch icons made operating the device very simple—so simple, in fact, that a child (or an alien creature) could do it. Urael had been able to match words with pictures and had learned to speak the human language all by himself. Though Urael came from a seemingly primitive culture, he was obviously very intelligent.

A voice crackled, "Captain!"

Kacey turned and saw K'Charr approaching, backed by four troopers armed with blasters. "Captain," K'Charr said, "is everything all right here?"

"Quite all right," the captain said. "One of the inhabitants of this world has introduced himself. Urael, this is K'Charr, my engineer."

K'Charr nodded stiffly, snorting blue fire into his bubble helmet.

"The peace of Kyrieh be with you, K'Charr," Urael said. "I have never seen a creature who breathes fire."

"That's just one of his many talents," the captain said. "Urael, I would like to meet—"

"Our people have no leader," Urael said. "We obey Kyrieh."

The captain looked surprised. "In that case—"

"I am sorry, Captain. I cannot take you to Kyrieh," Urael said. "Kyrieh is not in this place or that place. Kyrieh is in all places at once."

"But I—" the captain said.

"Thank you for your message of friendship from the Galactic Community," Urael said. "And thank you for offering us your machines, your science, and your medicines—but my people do not want these things."

Kacey was having trouble following the conversation. Urael seemed to be rejecting an offer her father hadn't even made yet. She looked at her father—and was startled to see that he appeared pale and shaken.

The captain took a deep breath, then said, "Would you mind—"

"Please," Urael said, "speak with your friends. I will wait here."

The captain led the landing party away from Urael. When they were far enough away that Urael couldn't overhear them, he said, "Did you notice anything strange about that conversation?"

"Urael seems kind of rude," Kacey said. "He's always interrupting!"

"He's not just interrupting," the captain said. "He knows everything I'm about to say before I say it. I was going to say, 'I would like to meet the leader of your people,' but I barely got two words out before Urael said, 'Our people have no leader.' Then I was about to say, 'In that case, I want to meet the one you call Kyrieh.' Again I only got two or three words out, and Urael interrupted and said, 'I cannot take you to Kyrieh.'"

"Captain," Maa Laas hooted, "are you saying Eréans haff power to read minds?"

Captain O'Quinn frowned. "Do you have a better explanation?"

Kacey felt a tingle of horror at the idea that an alien creature might be able to read her thoughts.

K'Charr shot a fiery glance in Urael's direction. "Captain," he said, "no other race in the galaxy has such powers. If the Eréans can read minds, it would be an incredible discovery. We need to know for sure."

Captain O'Quinn nodded. "I have a plan to find out."

Maa Laas bent closer to the captain. "What is plan?" she fluted.

The captain looked around at his crew. "My plan," he said, "is to ask him, 'Can you read my mind?'"

Kacey rolled her eyes. "Dad—I mean, Captain—this is serious!"

"I *am* serious," the captain said. "I'm going to ask Urael point blank and see what he tells me. After all, if he can read minds, he already knows what I'm thinking, so I might as well be honest."

Kacey had to agree with her father's logic.

"I'm also going to ask Urael to take a few of us to his village," the captain continued. "Along the way, I want you two, Cadet O'Quinn and Maa Laas, to engage Urael in conversation. Ask him questions. See if he can read your minds too. Okay, let's go."

They all went back to the place where Urael waited beside the row of graves. "Urael," the captain said. "Can you—"

"No, Captain," the Eréan said. "I do not have the ability to read your mind."

Urael agreed to guide them to his village, which was a ten-minute walk from the site of the wreck. Captain O'Quinn ordered K'Charr, the two techbots, and four of the troopers to remain with the wreckage and continue investigating. Taking the other four troopers with him, the captain set off toward the village with Kacey, Maa Laas, and Urael.

The Eréan led them along a winding path through the purple forest. As they went, Maa Laas paused frequently, using her scanner to gather information on the various plants that lined their path.

"Plant life on Eréa not like plants on Earth or Ankor Edge," she remarked. "Scanner shows plants haff pulse—they haff heartlike organ at base of plant that pumps life juices."

Kacey was fascinated with the trees of the purple forest. There were many different leaf shapes, fruit shapes, and trunk textures, but all were built on the same basic arrangement: A trunk grew out of a fat, bulb-shaped base that squatted on a root structure that looked like hundreds of strands of purple spaghetti. The trunks were slender and straight, ranging in color from purple to black. Clusters of leafy branches spread out from the bulbous top of each tree.

Some trees hung with clusters of jewel-like red berries, others with large pear-shaped orange fruit, and still others with massive yellow flowers. Kacey knew better than to sample any of the fruit. Though beautiful to look at, the fruit of Eréa might be poisonous to humans.

Kacey also saw many butterflylike creatures fluttering past, as big as birds, with wings that were bright yellow with red markings. There were orange-and-green striped worms on some of the plants, and on the ground were spiky purple creatures that looked a lot like sea anemones from the oceans of Earth.

"This place is like a Garden of Eden," Kacey said, her brown eyes shining with wonder.

She looked up at her dad. He looked different somehow. Aboard the starship, he was always grim and worried. But as he walked this forest pathway, a smile tugged at the corners of his mouth and he seemed almost at peace.

Urael looked at Kacey. "What is this Garden of Eden you talk of?" he asked.

"A beautiful place," Kacey said, "that existed a long time ago. Urael, do your people—"

"My people," Urael said, "love and obey the one you call God. We call him Kyrieh, the Creator of all. Everything comes from Kyrieh and returns to Kyrieh. He is before the beginning. He is after the end."

Kacey was stunned. She had planned to ask, "Do your people believe in God?" Urael had interrupted her and answered the very question that was on her mind!

"And what of the humans?" Urael said. "Do all human people believe in God?"

Kacey said, "Well, I—"

"Captain O'Quinn!" Urael said. The Eréan stopped in his tracks and stared at Kacey and her father. "Is it true what your daughter was about to say?"

"Is *what* true?" the captain said. "She didn't get to—"

"Your daughter was about to tell me," Urael said, "that she believes in God but you do not! Can this be true?"

The captain began, "I believe only in—"

"Yes!" Urael said. "I also believe only in what I see, hear, and know—but I have seen the light of Kyrieh! I have heard the voice of Kyrieh in my spirit! I have felt the joy of Kyrieh in my being! Every day I am fed by the hand of Kyrieh—what more proof is needed?"

"That's what I keep trying to tell my dad," Kacey said.

"How can this be," Urael said, "that the daughter is

wiser than the father? How can you be the captain, a ruler over others, when you say that Kyrieh, the All Creator, is not real? It is like saying two plus two equals zero! It is like seeing your face in a pool of water and then saying, 'I am not real!'"

The captain tried to stammer a reply, but Urael turned and looked at Maa Laas. "What of your people, Maa Laas?" Urael asked. "What do you believe about Kyrieh, about God?"

"We Ankoreans—" Maa Laas began.

"Have you explained all of this to Captain O'Quinn?" Urael asked. "Have you told him how the forces of creation are exactly balanced? Have you told him about the careful shaping of gravity? The controlled force of the creation explosion? Does he know that the chances of this universe happening by accident are less than one in a trillion trillion?"

"Maa Laas has—" the captain began.

"You admit that your own science officer has explained it to you, Captain," Urael said. "And still you claim Kyrieh is unreal! The Eréans know he is real, the Ankoreans know he is real, and your own daughter knows he is real. How can you say that God is not real?"

"My father doesn't believe in God," Kacey said, "because God let my mother die."

For several seconds no one spoke.

"Death," Urael finally said. "When I studied the computer, I learned the word *death*, but I didn't understand what it is. Now I know—a little. Those men we found in the wrecked flying craft—their bodies broken and not moving, their spirits gone. That was death, wasn't it? Kacey O'Quinn, is that what happened to your mother?"

Kacey's throat felt tight. "Yes," she said. "When she

died, my dad said, 'What kind of God would allow this to happen?'"

Urael's periscoping eyes bent toward Kacey. "And how did you answer your father?"

Kacey began, "I said—"

"Yes, of course," Urael said. "Though I do not understand death, I would give the same answer. All life comes from God. All life returns to God. But the love of God is unchanging."

"Do you mean to tell me—" the captain began.

"That is correct, Captain O'Quinn," Urael replied. "Before I saw the bodies of men on the wrecked flying vehicle, I never saw death before. Death is unknown on my world."

They continued on through the purple forest to Urael's village.

As the trees thinned around them on either side, Kacey smelled smoke—not a woodsy campfire smoke, but spicy smoke, like incense. The fragrance was sweet, with a hint of burnt cinnamon, plus a trace of something flowery, like jasmine petals. The ground sloped toward a clear and sparkling stream. A bridge of narrow planks and braided vines was suspended over the stream and anchored by pillars of weathered stone.

On the other side of the stream, Urael's village was spread out across a broad, sunny clearing. The village was a fanciful, colorful collection of tents and banners, with several fruit-laden tables under large awnings. The colors and shapes of the tents seemed randomly chosen, yet the village was beautifully harmonized with the purple hues of the surrounding forest.

In the center of the village, a bonfire burned within a ring of stones, sending a plume of thick, fragrant smoke straight up into a clear, blue-violet sky. Everywhere around the village were people just like Urael—tall, orchid-skinned people with periscoping eyes and tentacled fingers. Some were male, some were female, and some were children.

As Urael led the captain, Kacey, and the others across the bridge, he sang a high, clear song—at least, it sounded like music to Kacey's ears, though it was actually Eréan speech. Wherever they were, villagers stopped what they were doing and gathered around the strangers from space. They showed no trace of fear—just a polite, almost casual interest. The Eréans couldn't smile as humans do, since their mouths were vertical openings, yet something about the look in their eyes made Kacey feel welcomed and even loved.

Urael turned to the captain and said, "My people are eager to hear what you have to say. Talk, and I will tell them the meaning."

"Thank you," the captain said. He turned and faced the villagers. "People of Eréa, I come in peace—" he began.

Before he could say anything else, Urael sang something to his people in the Eréan language. The people replied in a chorus of musical voices. Then they all turned away and went about their business.

"Wait!" the captain said.

The villagers ignored him.

"Why are they leaving?" Kacey asked.

The captain turned to Urael. "Did I offend them?"

"They found your words quite pleasant," Urael said. "They told me to thank you for your generous offer of trade with your Galactic Community, but they are not interested in your machines and goods. Our answer is no."

"What offer?" Captain O'Quinn spluttered. "I hardly even—"

"I told them exactly what you were about to say," Urael said. "'People of Eréa, I come in peace, representing the ten races of the Galactic Community. I offer you the friendship of our community and the benefits of our trading partnerships and advanced technology.' Aren't those the words you were about to say, Captain O'Quinn?"

"That's exactly what I was going to say," the captain said. "Word for word. You still say you can't read my mind?"

"I assure you, I cannot," Urael said, his pale eyes blinking innocently on twin eyestalks. "I do not know why you keep asking me that."

The captain, Kacey, Maa Laas, and the four troopers spent an hour in the village. Maa Laas spider-walked from tent to tent with her scanner, recording every aspect of Eréan village life. The captain and Urael sat under a brightly colored awning and carried on a strange conversation. The captain would speak two or three words of a question, and Urael would interrupt and give a long answer.

Kacey walked around the village, trying to communicate with the Eréan people by smiling, pointing, and gesturing. Finally she went to see how her father was getting along with Urael. She found her father sitting in the shade, eyeing the alien with a grumpy, frustrated expression.

"But what about—" the captain began.

"We do not need your medicines, Captain," Urael said. "Our people never get sick."

"I don't—"

"Why don't you believe me, Captain?" Urael said. "I

would not tell you an unreal thing. Here there is no disease, no death."

"But what about—"

"What you call 'old age' is unknown here," Urael said. "Yes, we live long compared to you humans. I have seen more than nine hundred summers. My father—" Urael pointed to an Eréan who was adding wood to the smoky fire—"he has seen more than a thousand summers. And his father, who lives in the next village, is older still."

Kacey looked at the Eréan who was carrying wood. That was Urael's father? He looked as young and healthy as Urael himself! Kacey knew that an Eréan year was slightly longer than a year on Earth. According to Urael, the people of Eréa were still in the prime of life after living for ten centuries or more.

"But what about—" her father began.

"No, Captain," Urael said, "our world never has too many people. Children are born every season, but there are never too many people. You see, for each of us, a time comes when Kyrieh calls us to himself. When he calls, we make a journey through the sea to an island. A great light is there, the Light of Kyrieh. We walk into the light. Beyond that light is Kyrieh's great village, where never is night."

"But that's—"

"No, Captain," Urael said. "That is not death. On our world, the spirit never leaves the body."

"But why—"

"I do not know," Urael said, "why there is death in your world and no death in mine. It may have to do with the Choice."

When Kacey heard Urael say "the Choice," she could almost sense that the word should be capitalized, as if "the Choice" was a special event in Eréan history.

"What was—" Kacey began.

"A long time ago," Urael said, "Kyrich gave the first Eréans a choice: love Kyrieh or reject him. They chose the love. If the first Eréans had made a different choice, we also might know this death thing. Maybe someone once made a choice for the human people. Maybe that is why your people die."

"It's true," Kacey said. "The first humans made a choice of their own."

"An unhappy choice?" Urael asked.

"A very unhappy choice," Kacey said.

"Captain," a high, fluting voice said. Kacey and her father turned and saw Maa Laas approaching.

"Yes?" the captain said.

"I haff scanned all fillagers," Maa Laas said. "All seem healthy, no sickness or old age. Plenty of food here. Is like story from Earth. Is like Garden of Eden—but without snake."

The captain nodded. His eyes were troubled.

"One more thing," Maa Laas added. "Fire in middle of fillage—always it burns, always it smokes, but fire has no purpose."

"No purpose?" the captain said.

"Fire not used for light or heat or cooking," the science officer said. "People of purple planet burn wood with much waxy resin. Makes sweet smoke, but fire has no purpose."

The captain turned to Urael. "Why—"

"We make smoke," Urael answered, "because Kyrieh says, 'Make smoke.'"

"But why did Kyrieh—"

"We don't know why," Urael said. "Kyrieh knows. That is enough."

The captain silently considered this information for a few

moments, then he put his wrist com to his lips. "Captain to K'Charr," he said.

"K'Charr here, Captain," the Krematian engineer's voice crackled in response.

"How much power remaining in your oven suit?"

"Two point eight hours, Captain. Still plenty of safety margin."

The captain nodded. "How is the crash investigation coming? Any idea what caused those engine pods to explode?"

"It's still a mystery, Captain. Never saw anything like it."

"We're leaving the village now," the captain said, "and we'll rejoin you in ten minutes. Captain out."

"I will guide you, Captain," Urael said. "I do not want you to get lost in the forest."

Urael, the captain, Kacey, Maa Laas, and the troopers crossed the bridge and entered the forest. Kacey walked beside Urael, ahead of the others.

"There's something I don't understand," she said. "Whenever we ask a question—"

"I am puzzled too," Urael said. "Among my people, it is polite to interrupt when another person talks so that no words are wasted. But your father does not like to be interrupted. When you humans talk to each other, you talk all the words. When you listen, you listen to all the words. That made me think, 'Why do the sky people make me waste words?' Your thinking and Eréan thinking are very different thinkings."

"That's for sure!" Kacey said.

"Your thinking is stuck," Urael said, "like a stick poked in the riverbank. Eréan thinking floats like a leaf upon the stream."

Kacey turned Urael's words over in her mind, trying to

make sense of them. She glanced back over her shoulder to see if her father was listening, but he was talking to Maa Laas.

"Kacey," Urael said, "your father believes I hear his thinking while it is in his head, but I do not. He thinks I am telling him an unreal thing—"

"An 'unreal thing'?" Kacey said. "Oh, you mean a lie."

"Yes," Urael said. "He thinks I am telling a lie, but I am not. Only Kyrieh knows the thinkings inside the head."

A short time later, Urael, Kacey, the captain, Maa Laas, and the four troopers reached the landing site. They found K'Charr and the rest of the landing party beside the waiting transport.

The captain said to K'Charr, "It'll take an hour and fifty minutes to reach *Far Encounter*. That gives you a forty-five-minute safety cushion for the power on your oven suit."

Kacey turned to Urael. "Good-bye, Urael," she said. "Maybe I'll come back someday."

"I have heard the voice of Kyrieh in my spirit," Urael said. "When you leave this world, you will not come back."

Kacey's heart sank.

"It's time to go, Kacey," the captain said, placing his hands on her shoulders. He turned to the rest of the landing party and thumbed toward the boarding ramp. "Everybody aboard," he said.

The orchid-skinned creature turned and walked slowly toward the purple forest.

The two techbots, Wilbur and Orville, were the first to

climb the boarding ramp. K'Charr and Maa Laas followed. Captain O'Quinn and Kacey started up the ramp as the troopers waited on the grass, weapons at the ready.

Kacey and her father were halfway up the ramp when they heard a shout behind them: "Stop!" They turned and saw Urael running toward the transport. The eight troopers stepped forward, raising their blasters.

"Hold it right there!" shouted one of the troopers. "Don't move!"

Urael stopped in his tracks. "Captain O'Quinn!" he shouted. "If you go up in the air, I will see that you all die!"

The captain started back down, his boots clanking angrily on the steel ramp. "What is this? A threat?"

"*Threat?*" Urael said. "I don't know this word. I only know that if you try to leave, I will see that you all die!"

"Do you think I need your permission to—"

"Captain, I do not know this word *permission*. I only know that if you fly away, I will see that you all die! I will see that your vehicle explodes in fire, smoke, and thunder! None will survive."

Kacey heard all this from halfway up the boarding ramp. "Dad!" she called. "There must be some misunderstanding! Urael wouldn't—"

"Into the transport, cadet!" her father snapped. "That's an order!"

Kacey turned and trudged up the ramp. She was sure her father was making a big mistake—and she had to do something about it.

The captain turned to Urael. "Get away from this transport!" he said. "We're taking off whether you like it or not!"

"Captain," said a deep, rumbling voice behind him.

The captain glanced over his shoulder and saw K'Charr

coming down the ramp. "Cadet O'Quinn said there was trouble down here."

"This . . . this *creature* is threatening to destroy our ship if we take off," the captain said.

"Destroy our ship? Impossible," K'Charr said. "He has no weapons of any kind."

The captain glared fiercely at Urael. "Maybe he has weapons we don't know about," he said.

Inside the transport, Kacey knelt next to the top of the ramp, straining to hear the discussion below. Heart pounding, she prayed. She was sure that the crisis was all due to some horrible misunderstanding. Though her father thought Urael was a liar who could read their minds, Kacey trusted the orchid-skinned creature. There had to be some logical explanation.

Yet she had heard Urael's words. They certainly sounded like a threat.

And what did her father mean when he said, "Maybe he has weapons we don't know about"?

"Troopers," the captain said, "keep your blasters on him. Don't fire unless I give the order."

Eight troopers aimed their photon blasters at Urael.

The captain took K'Charr aside. "Urael said our transport would explode 'in fire, smoke, and thunder'—his exact words." He pointed to the wreckage of the other transport. "And fire, smoke, and thunder is what happened to the hijacked transport."

"But, Captain," K'Charr said, "how can Urael attack a transport without weapons?"

"Maybe his *mind* is a weapon," the captain said. "Psychokinesis."

"Mind over matter?" K'Charr snorted fire. "Impossible! There is no such thing! Surely, you don't believe in such fairy tales!"

"Look," the captain said, "we already know that Urael can read minds, right? And a creature with the ability to read minds may have other mental powers as well—such as the power to destroy a transport by thought energy alone. We may be forced to shoot him, if only to save ourselves."

"But Urael wouldn't hurt us!" said a voice behind the captain.

The captain whirled and saw his daughter coming down the ramp.

"Kace!" the captain said. "Cadet O'Quinn, I told you to wait in the—"

"Yes, sir! You did, sir!" Kacey said. "But you're making a terrible mistake! *Please* don't hurt Urael!"

"Silence, cadet!" the captain snarled.

Kacey's mouth snapped shut.

Captain O'Quinn strode to the place where the troopers guarded Urael at gunpoint. Raising his wrist com to his lips, the captain said, "Captain to *Far Encounter*."

"*Far Encounter* here, Captain," an electronic voice crackled from the wrist com. "Techbot Sparks in temporary command."

"Sparks," the captain said, eyeing Urael as he spoke, "our lives have been threatened by one of the inhabitants of this planet. His village is located about a mile due west of our present location."

"I have the village located, Captain," Sparks said.

"Sparks," the captain said, "if we don't make it safely back to the starship, you are ordered to train the ship's photon blasters on that village and blow it out of existence. Is that clear?"

"Understood, Captain."

The captain glared at Urael. "Do you understand the order I just gave my crew?" Again Urael tried to interrupt, but the captain continued talking. "We are returning to our ship. If we are harmed in any way, the starship *Far Encounter* will destroy your village—and everyone in it."

"Captain O'Quinn," Urael said, "if you destroy my people, they will return to Kyrieh. But if you go up in the sky, I will see that you all die in fire, smoke, and thunder."

The captain stared in amazement at Urael. Then he said, "Everyone in the transport. We lift off in five minutes."

"What?" Kacey said as the others moved toward the ramp.

"We're leaving," the captain said. "K'Charr's oven suit is running out of power. If we don't leave now, my engineer will freeze to death."

"But Urael said—" Kacey began.

"He's bluffing," the captain said. "He won't attack us. He knows that if we are harmed, his village will be wiped out. Now get inside the transport, Kacey."

"I will see that you die, Captain!" Urael shouted, backing away from the transport. "Fire, smoke, thunder! I will see that you all die!"

Kacey strapped herself into her seat and looked out the quartz view port. She saw Urael standing at the edge of the clearing, shouting and gesturing. *Think, Kacey!* she told herself.

She was sure her father was wrong about Urael's ability to read minds—and his ability to use his mind as a weapon. There had to be some other explanation for Urael's threat to blow up the transport—

Or *was* it a threat?

What had Urael said? *I will see that you all die! I will see that your vehicle explodes in fire, smoke, and thunder!* Did Urael mean, "I will kill you"? Or did he mean, "I will see your death take place"? Though Urael had learned human language, he hadn't fully mastered it. Some of his sentences were awkwardly phrased. Maybe Urael wasn't threatening them at all. Maybe he was trying to warn them of danger!

If Urael was trying to warn them that their transport would blow up, how did he know it was going to happen?

Kacey tried to remember everything Urael had told her. What was that remark he made about Eréan thinking and human thinking? *Your thinking is stuck, like a stick poked in the riverbank. Eréan thinking floats like a leaf upon the stream.* What did that mean?

Your thinking is stuck.

If human thinking was stuck, then Eréan thinking was *not* stuck—whatever that meant.

Eréan thinking floats like a leaf upon the stream.

Was Urael talking about the stream of time? Was he saying that Eréans experienced time differently from humans?

God, she prayed, *please make this clear to me! Please help me understand before it's too late!*

In the cockpit, Wilbur and Orville prepared the craft for takeoff. Kacey had flown on transports many times, and she knew the routine for vertical takeoffs. The tech-

The Science behind the Story

Anthro . . . Whatever

When Kacey and other members of the landing party walk through the purple forest to Urael's village, they discuss the existence of God. Maa Laas, the Ankorean science officer, begins to tell Urael about a series of amazing features in the universe that indicate that the universe was *intelligently designed*.

People have always seen God's hand in creation. But in 1973 physicist Brandon Carter invented the term *anthropic principle* (from *anthropos*, the Greek word for humanity). According to Carter's anthropic principle, the universe appears to be "fine-tuned" or deliberately designed to bring forth life—including human life. And if just one of these many features in the universe were slightly out of balance, life couldn't exist!

Here are just a few of those fine-tuned features. You don't have to understand them all to see how they all point to God:

The strong nuclear force, the weak nuclear force, gravity, and the electromagnetic force are all delicately balanced to allow the creation of the elements needed for life, such as carbon and oxygen.

The complex relationship between helium atoms and beryllium atoms (say that ten times fast) enables carbon to exist. So what? Carbon is the building block of life. If this relationship was off

by as little as 1 percent, the life-giving element of carbon could not exist.

The list goes on and on: the neutron-proton mass relationship, the neutrino mass, the polarity of water molecules, the dimensional structure of the universe, the ripples in the big bang (or, as some like to call it, the initial creation event), and dozens and dozens of other "coincidental" features.

More and more scientists are seeing how things all appear to be carefully engineered to produce life. And if they're engineered, that means there's an engineer. Now does it make sense? In other words, God's fingerprints are all over the universe! But Kacey knew that already.

bots would fire the belly-side thrusters, propelling the transport off the ground. Once the transport had cleared the trees, the engine pods would fire, launching the craft forward.

If you fly away, I will see that you all die! I will see that your vehicle explodes in fire, smoke, and thunder! None will survive.

Kacey gasped! She remembered the engine pods of the wrecked transport. They had both exploded in "fire, smoke, and thunder." Suddenly, she knew—something would happen to the transport's engine pods the moment they were fired. Urael was telling the truth. He was trying to warn them about a defect in the engine pods.

Now she had to convince her father—or they would all die!

She felt the transport shudder, and she was pressed into her seat. The transport leaped into the air on a blast from the belly-side thrusters.

Kacey screamed! "Dad! No! Don't fire the engine pods!"

she shouted toward the cockpit, leaning against her seat restraints. "Urael was telling the truth! He wasn't threatening us! He was *warning* us!"

Her father turned at the sound of her screams. "Cadet O'Quinn!" he snapped.

"Dad, listen!" she said. "If we fire the engine pods, we'll die—just like Urael said!"

"Kace—"

"Dad!" Kacey babbled on, expecting the transport to explode at any instant. "Our minds are stuck in the now! But the Eréans can look forward! Dad, Urael doesn't read minds! He reads the future! He knew what you were going to say before you said it because he could look into the future! And he knows that this transport is going to explode because he already saw it happening! Dad! Please don't—"

"Kacey," her father said. "We're on the ground."

Kacey stopped babbling. "We are?" she said weakly—then she looked out the view port. It was true. The transport was back on the ground.

"I believe you, Kacey," her father said.

It took K'Charr and the two techbots fifteen minutes to remove the cover panels from the two engine pods. "Look at that!" the Krematian engineer growled as he and Orville set the portside cover panels on the purple grass. "Just like the starboard engine! What a mess!"

Kacey stood on tiptoe and looked into the innards of the engine pod—a complex collection of housings, chambers, and tubes. The front of the engine was coated with globs of foaming black goo.

"K'Charr," Kacey said, "what's that bubbly black stuff?"

The engineer's breath flamed. "That," he said, "is what's left of the carbon-carbon vector baffle. It's a good thing you spoke up when you did. If Wilbur had kicked in the engine pods, we would have blown sky high—just like the other transport."

Kacey shuddered to think how close they had come.

K'Charr reached into the engine housing and pulled out a gooey blob of the dissolved vector baffle. "I've never seen anything like this," he said. "This baffle was made of woven fibers of nanocrystalline diamond—made to withstand temperatures of almost six thousand degrees! Look at it now!" He rubbed the piece between the fingers of his lower right hand, and it left sticky black carbon smears on the glove of his oven suit.

A few yards away, Maa Laas crouched over her scanner while Captain O'Quinn and Urael stood behind her, watching. "Theory confirmed, Captain," he hooted. "Look at scanner."

The captain grunted. "The air of this planet is filled with microbes that feed on pure carbon."

"Yes," Maa Laas said. "Microbes live off soot from fillage bonfires. Soot is almost pure carbon."

Kacey said, "That explains one thing Urael told us. He said Kyrieh commanded the Eréan people to keep those fires burning night and day, but Urael didn't know the reason for that command. Now we know at least part of the reason. The bonfires put soot in the air to feed the microbes, and the microbes consume the soot to clean the air. It must have something to do with balancing the ecology of the planet."

"Correct," Maa Laas said. "Microbes perform photosynthesis, like plants on Earth. Microbes eat carbon, combine carbon with hydrogen and oxygen, and make trisaccharide, complex hydrocarbon, as waste product."

"Trisaccharide?" Kacey said, remembering her basic chemistry. "That's a sugar, isn't it?"

"Correct," Maa Laas said. "Sugar rains down on planet, feeds purple 'plants,' which are not true plants at all. Purple plants have no chloroplasts to photosynthesize like Earth plants. That's why carbon-eating microbes essential to life cycle of purple planet. Microbes make trisaccharide food for purple plants."

"Those microbes usually feed on tiny soot particles for carbon," the captain said. "But when those microbes discovered the pure carbon fibers in our engine pods, they had themselves a real feast—and they multiplied like crazy."

"I'll call the ship," K'Charr said. "I'll have the fabricating shop make a new set of vector baffles from zirconium-yttrium oxide fibers—works almost as well, but there's no carbon for those little bugs to chew on. The new baffles can be dropped to us by atmosphere probe in three hours."

"That still leaves us with a big problem," the captain said. "The new vector baffles will arrive in time to save the rest of us—but what about you? Your oven suit runs out of energy in about two hours."

"Doesn't he have a spare oven suit on the ship?" Kacey asked.

"He does," the captain said, "but we can't get it down here. It won't fit into an atmosphere probe."

Kacey gasped. "But if we don't get back to the ship, he'll freeze to death!"

The Krematian sighed, exhaling a shimmer of blue flames into his bubble helmet. "I had hoped to die of old age," K'Charr said, "about two hundred years from now. But if I must perish, Captain, at least I've had the privilege of serving at your side."

A grim moment of silence passed.

"Why must the burning creature perish?" Urael asked. "Can we not build a fire for K'Charr to keep his blood hot until you fix your vehicle?"

The captain blinked in surprise, then turned to his engineer. "K'Charr," he said, "would it work? Would a bonfire keep you from freezing to death?"

"You want me to sit in a bonfire?" K'Charr said.

"We could shut down your oven suit," the captain said, "and build a fire around you. That would save your suit power for the trip back to the starship. You'd have just enough power to make it."

K'Charr's glowing eyes widened. "Yes!" he said. "It should work."

"I will gather wood for the fire," Urael said.

"I'll help," Kacey said.

Urael and Kacey hurried toward the forest together. Five minutes later they were back with armloads of the sweet-smelling resin wood—the same wood used in the bonfire in Urael's village. Kacey and Urael arranged the wood. One of the troopers lit the fire with a shot from his photon blaster. As the fire blazed up, K'Charr peeled off his oven suit and leaped into the fire.

Kacey and Urael dashed off for more wood. One of the troopers took a shovel out of the transport and the squad of troopers took turns ladling hot embers over K'Charr's head and shoulders. "I'm too hot in front," K'Charr grumbled, "and I'm freezing in back! More coals! Not in my face, you lunkhead! Down my back!"

Soon Kacey and Urael returned and dumped another load of firewood next to the bonfire. Then they stood beside the captain and watched the troopers shovel coals of fire over the Krematian's rugged black hide.

"I'm worried about one thing," Kacey said. "We must have those carbon-eating microbes all over us. What if we take them back with us? If they got loose on another planet, they could cause an ecological disaster!"

"Every member of the landing party will have to be nano-decontaminated and quarantined," the captain said. "We'll also have to sterilize the transport when we get to the docking bay. But Maa Laas says the carbon-eating microbes are easily destroyed. It shouldn't be a problem."

"Oh no!" Kacey said. "Our bodies are 20 percent carbon! What if those microbes are eating us up inside right now?"

"Maa Laas told me the microbes like only *pure* carbon," the captain said. "The carbon in our bodies is in compounds like carbohydrates, carbonates, fats, proteins, and nucleic acids. Don't worry, Kace. You don't taste good to those little bugs."

"That's a relief," Kacey said. "But I guess we can never return to this planet, can we? Because of the microbes, I mean."

"That's right," the captain said. "I'm going to recommend to Space Fleet command that this planet be placed permanently off-limits to space travel. Eréa may look like Eden, but it's a shipwreck planet—dangerous to space travelers. And if future—"

"A wise decision, Captain," Urael interrupted. "As you were going to say, if future space travelers accidentally carried my planet's microbes to other worlds, great harm would follow."

"That reminds me," the captain said, frowning at Urael. "Kacey tried to explain to me how you always know what I'm going to say even before I say it, but I still don't—"

"It's really quite simple," Urael said, interrupting as usual. "Human minds—and Ankorean minds and Krematian minds—are stuck in time, locked in the now. But Eréans experience time in a different way. My mind can float along the time stream. I can see now, and I can see later all at once. I can hear your words before you say them—that's why I answer you before you finish speaking. You see? Simple."

"Yeah," the captain said, scratching his head. "Simple. But if—"

"That too is easy to understand, Captain. When I hear you say what you are going to say before you say it, then I can answer what you are going to say, and that saves you the trouble of saying it, and it saves me the trouble of hearing you say it twice. You see?"

"Yes," the captain said. "Well, actually, no. The thing I don't understand is . . ." His shoulders sagged. "I'm not even sure how to ask the question."

"I think I know," Kacey said. "You want to know how Urael can know what you're about to say when he keeps interrupting you before you can say it. If he interrupts you, then he really didn't see the future. He *changed* the future by interrupting you, because he kept you from saying what he heard you were going to say."

The captain nodded uncertainly. "Yeah. I think that's—"

"Again, it's very simple to explain," Urael said. "When I see the future, I do not see a future that *must* be, only a future that will be unless it is changed by someone's choice. Kyrieh has given humans, Ankoreans, Krematians, and Eréans the ability to make choices that change what will be—yet Kyrieh always controls the outcome. Captain, when I saw your flying vehicle explode in the future, I knew that you could choose to change the future so that you wouldn't have to die. That's why I begged you to make a different choice."

"And when you said—" the captain began.

"Exactly," Urael replied. "When I told you, 'I will see

that you all die,' I meant that my mind had floated ahead in time. In my mind, I had already seen your vehicle explode. I did not want to see it again with my eyes."

"So what you meant was—" the captain began.

"Ah!" Urael said, his tentacled fingers waving in a gesture of sudden understanding. "The words you were about to speak have made me wiser! Captain, I spoke your language brokenly. When I said, 'I will see that you all die,' you thought I was saying I would *cause* your death! Captain, I would never do such a thing! I would never break the law of Kyrieh!"

The captain groaned and put his head in his hands. "When you explain it to me," he said, "it almost makes sense—but just when I think I'm getting it, my head starts to hurt." He looked up at Urael. "Anyway, Urael, I know now that you would never do anything to harm me or my people. I'm sorry I misjudged you."

"Don't feel bad," Urael said. "Captain, we Eréans have three hearts—and my three hearts overflow with gladness that you did not die."

The captain looked over at Kacey and grinned. "We're just lucky my daughter figured it out in time," he said.

"It wasn't luck, Dad," Kacey said. "We're alive because of answered prayer."

The captain shrugged. "I guess I'll have to think about that."

"Captain," Urael said, "I will talk to Kyrieh, and I will ask him to enlarge your understanding."

Just then they heard Orville's electronic shout—"Heads up! Probe arriving!" The techbot pointed skyward.

Kacey looked up and saw the probe—a speck against the blue-violet sky—falling straight toward them. As it fell, a brilliant white parachute blossomed. The probe landed with pinpoint accuracy ten meters from the transport.

Wilbur and Orville rushed to the probe, a rocket-shaped tube about a meter long. They pried open its side panel and pulled out the replacement vector baffles and began installing them in the engine pods.

"Well," the captain said, "we'll be leaving soon."

Teardrops sparkled in Kacey's eyes. "I won't ever see you again, Urael," she said.

"We will see each other again," Urael said, "in Kyrieh's village of light." With one tentacle, he brushed away a tear that slid down Kacey's face. "This water from your eyes," he said. "I have never seen such a thing before."

Kacey had to laugh, even as she cried. "It's a teardrop," she said.

"A teardrop," Urael said, holding up his moistened tentacle, examining the liquid bead that glistened like a jewel in the sunlight. "We do not have teardrops on my world."

"Where I come from," Kacey said, "we have lots of them."

"I will remember you always, Kacey O'Quinn," Urael said, "and I will talk to Kyrieh about you every day." Urael reached out and wrapped his tentacles around Kacey, enfolding her in a hug.

The captain grimaced to see those tentacles around his daughter, but Kacey didn't mind. She hugged Urael tightly, crying openly.

"Captain!" Wilbur said. "Orville and I have completed repairs. We are ready to lift off."

The captain and Kacey walked toward the transport. K'Charr was out of the bonfire and back in his oven suit, standing by the boarding ramp.

"Engineer," the captain said, "I trust you came through your fiery ordeal without ill effects."

K'Charr gestured toward the troopers. "Those lunkheads

got ashes inside my oven suit!" he growled, spouting blue flames. "I'll have a cinder rash by the time we reach the ship."

"As long as you're well enough to gripe," the captain said, "I'm not worried."

The space travelers boarded the transport. Kacey took her seat by the quartz view port and looked out. Urael was standing by the edge of the forest, watching and waiting. Moments later the thrusters fired, and billows of white smoke hid Urael from Kacey's eyes. When the smoke cleared, she could see nothing below but the purple horizon.

Bending his eyestalks skyward, Urael watched the transport shrink to a speck and then vanish among the clouds. The space travelers were gone.

Urael looked down at the tip of his tentacle. Kacey's teardrop still glittered there. Treasuring that drop of moisture as if it were a precious jewel, Urael turned and started down the path that led through the purple forest.

As he walked, he felt a strange feeling in all three of his hearts, something he had never felt before. At first, he was baffled by it. Then he realized what that feeling in his hearts meant.

And he began to understand the teardrop.

Something seemed to be distracting our master storyteller. His eyebrows climbed up and down his forehead like hamsters in an exercise wheel. Finally he said, "My young friends, I believe it's time we headed back to the hub. But there's plenty more to see there."

I found myself walking behind Amy but watching Talismort ahead of her. He was kind, but he was mysterious. Where did he come from? What was he doing way out here? And how had he traveled to all the places he was telling us about?

On our way back, we took yet another walkway. I noticed that one of the pearl lights was out. As Talismort passed through the shadow, he seemed to disappear for a moment. Amy was watching the floor in front of her. She didn't see. Did I? Or was it my imagination? It was at that moment that I realized how tired my eyes were. So much to see here.

"It gets a little lonely being inside a place where you can't go outside for a walk," Talismort called over his shoulder. "Outside these walls is a hostile place indeed. No air. So cold that you'd freeze solid in short order." He stiffened and stopped in his tracks. He held up a finger, pointing at the ceiling, and turned toward us. "Then again, there are places where you wouldn't want to go outside anyway. Places where people stay inside during the day, as afraid of what's in the light as they are of their nightmares in the dark. I know of such a place."

·········1·2·········

Topside

John B. Olson

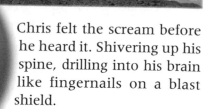

Chris felt the scream before he heard it. Shivering up his spine, drilling into his brain like fingernails on a blast shield.

"No . . ." He spun around, sweeping the rust-colored terrain with wide, staring eyes. The scream sounded again, this time louder. There it was, near the edge of the crater. A shifting blur. The glow of pale green eyes.

Goliathon! Chris dove for cover behind a mushroom-shaped rock, but his leap sent him too high. He sailed over the rock in a giant slow-motion arc and smacked helmet first into the rocky soil. "Stupid planet . . ." Arms and legs flailing, he rebounded off the ground and flipped over onto his back.

A low growl rumbled through his feedback suit. The tremor of distant steps. It had spotted him. He was as good as dead.

"So much for my mission." He scrambled to his feet and plunged up a broad, rocky slope, skipping and jumping almost four meters into the air. Another roar, louder now. A backward glance confirmed his fears. The Goliathon was gaining on him. The nearest airlock was almost a kilometer away. He'd never make it.

Checking the location indicator on the sleeve of his feedback suit, Chris topped the rise and set out across a sandy plain. His legs felt like rubber, and his suit chafed at his elbows and knees, but still he kept on running. A Goliathon—three metric tons of muscle, teeth, and poison-laced claws. If he could just reach the airlock. If he could just get inside . . .

Finally, after what seemed an eternity, a glass dome peeked out over the top of a shifting dune. The airlock! He was going to make it. As long as the hatch wasn't sealed . . .

He pounded up the sand dune and almost slammed into a gold-suited figure. A boy about his age. A blue three was stamped on his chest. Third level. He wouldn't last a millisecond.

Chris pressed the communications link on his wrist without breaking stride. "Goliathon. Right behind me. Quick, get inside!" He skidded to a stop in front of the airlock and spun the wheel on the massive hatch, cracking the door open. He wriggled inside. "Come on. Hurry! It's right behind us!"

Silence. Chris turned back to the door. What was taking him so long? He peeked his head outside and looked around. The guy was gone.

"Hey, did you hear me?" Chris jabbed at the switch of

his com link. "Goliathon!" He double-checked the power level of his transmitter. Green and steady. What was wrong with that guy? He stepped through the airlock door and hesitated. It was too late now. There wasn't anything he could do. Besides, if the guy was stupid enough to—

An ear-splitting roar rattled the hatch. Faster than thought, Chris was scrambling down the dune, laser rifle unsheathed and gripped like a lance in both hands. The goliathon, with its glinting scales and angular serpentine face, was crouched at the bottom of the slope. Its flaming eyes were narrowed in an expression of demonic rage. It turned on him, rearing back onto its hind legs. Its enormous, talon-studded claw gripped a limp gold suit.

Too late. Chris was about to run back up the dune, when a gold flash caught his eye. The suit was still struggling. The Goliathon was just playing with the guy.

Chris dropped to the ground and squeezed off a shot at the hulking beast. Another shot right between the gleaming eyes. Another!

The goliathon's howl of rage hit Chris full in the chest, rattling through his bones. The beast leaped at him with bared fangs, knocking the rifle from his grip. Razor-sharp claws glinted in the pale peach light, and a crushing blow sent him sailing through the air. He saw flashing red lights, the only indication of pain he had ever known. And then darkness. Cold, black death.

"No!" Chris struggled to his feet and paced the grid-lined floor of the game's holding station. "Of all the stupid . . ." He pressed a switch on his wrist and scanned the display that appeared on the walls. His account was down to almost nothing. The death had cost him fifty credits.

"What was I thinking?" He pulled off his sensor gloves and unzipped his jacket.

So much for his great idea. Reaching out to others . . .

Some mission. Life just didn't work like that anymore. Maybe in Bible times, but not in the twenty-first century. He was out of the game for the rest of the day—for the rest of the month if his parents didn't give him an advance on his allowance.

How was he supposed to reach out with an empty account? He felt behind his head and loosened the straps that secured his visor screen. "That guy didn't even know I was a Christian. I wasted fifty credits."

A voice sounded in Chris's ear just as he was about to pull the visor off.

"Hello?" He pressed it back into place and swung around.

The guy in the gold suit was standing there watching him through dark, puffy eyes.

"Yeah?"

The boy looked away. "I uh . . . You saved my life back there. I . . . really appreciate it."

"No problem." Chris fumbled with the strap of his visor, wondering if he should say something about the fifty credits.

"I was thinking . . ." The guy kicked at an invisible tether on the floor. "I thought maybe . . . if you didn't mind, maybe we could party up for an excursion or something. I'm only third level on this site, but I'm twenty-six on Lost Colony. Ever play Lost Colony?"

"Sorry." Chris shook his head. "I'd really like to, but I was just about to switch off."

"No problem." The guy looked down at his feet. "Maybe some other time?"

"Sure," Chris said. "Another time." He reached for his visor.

"I'm Joel."

"What?"

"Joel Knight. That's my name."

"Your *real* name?" Chris eyed the guy suspiciously. Why would he give out his real name?

Joel nodded and cleared his throat. "If you don't mind me asking . . . I thought maybe . . . What's your name? Maybe we could trade messages."

"DeathSting99420."

Joel nodded. "I'm MarsColony3009." His eyes darkened. "Are you sure you don't want to party up? We could play Book Reader or Penal Colony Twelve or maybe—"

"Look, I'd really like to, but . . ." Chris tinted his visor to filter out the color he felt rising to his cheeks. "Truth is, I'm almost out of credits. I've barely got enough to—" A warning chime sounded in his ears. He had less than half an hour left in the holding station. "Look, I'm getting dinged now. I've got to switch off." He reached for his wrist controller.

"I could transfer you credits!" Joel stepped forward. "I've got plenty. We could go through a broker. I wouldn't even have to know the name on your account."

Chris shook his head. "My parents don't allow me to do transfers."

"Parents?" Joel's eyes went wide. "As in more than one?"

"Yeah, a mom and a dad. You?"

"I've got a mom, but . . ." Joel's voice trailed off. "But I haven't seen her in months. She's in quarantine now. Contracted a rhinovirus."

"A cold?" Chris tried to keep the skepticism out of his voice. "How'd she catch a cold?"

"She was in New Boston during the outbreak. Just so happens it's the only Mars colony left that doesn't use the new air filters."

Chris nodded. The New Boston outbreak had been in

the news for weeks. "So with your mom gone, who's keeping you safe?"

"Nobody." Joel let out a sigh. "They set up a Guardian program. I've been on my own for almost a month."

Chris winced at the emotion in his voice. "They say . . . uh . . . I heard turning the Guardian's volume off makes it less lonely."

"Believe me, I tried. It doesn't help." Joel lowered his eyes. He looked miserable.

"So . . ." Chris tried to think of something else to say. Something happier. "So you're playing from New Boston?"

"Olympia 32 . . ."

"No way! That's where I live." Chris spoke into his wrist controller, and a map of Olympia appeared on the wall. "What are your coordinates?"

Joel shrugged and turned slowly away from the wall.

"Sorry," Chris said. "Forget it. I shouldn't have asked."

"No, it's okay." Joel looked down at his controller and punched in a series of keys. "I just had to check. I'm right here." He pressed his screen, and a red arrow appeared on the map.

"No way!" Chris stepped toward the map. The arrow was right next to his bunker. "We're practically on top of each other! I can't believe it. It's almost like we were meant—" The room dimmed, and Chris's head rang with a chorus of bells. His time was almost up. Creating the map had used up too many credits.

"Look, I've got to switch off, but I've got an idea. My parents won't be home till late. Maybe we could go topside and finish this conversation."

"Topside?" Joel's eyes bulged. "You mean a meeting? Person to person?"

"Why not? It'd be way more exciting than Lost Colony."

"But we can't. I mean . . . It's too dangerous. We could get killed."

"At least the death wouldn't cost fifty credits."

"I'm serious. My mom would kill me if I ever went topside. I don't even have an encounter suit."

"But I've got one. Wait at your airlock. I'll be right there."

"But you can't. It's too—"

The chamber went suddenly dark. Glowing letters filled Chris's vision. "Session interrupted. Please add more credits to your account."

He pulled off his visor and squirmed out of his feedback suit, struggling against the tangle of force lines that kept the suit centered in the heavily padded rec room.

Joel Knight . . . What were the odds? He'd never met anyone who lived so close. They were practically in the same complex. It was a miracle. He'd decided to try to reach out and then, poof. God had given him his chance. His parents would understand. They had to understand.

Chris ran to the airlock cabinets and pulled out his encounter suit. The silver material sparkled like data crystals in the soft overhead light. He'd almost forgotten how beautiful it was. His father had bought it second-hand at an adventuring site almost a year ago. They'd meant to go out exploring together, but life had gotten so busy with school programs and Lost Colony and his Adventure Guild membership. He'd tried it on a couple of times, but he'd never actually made it topside. It was going to be great!

He stepped into the pants and heavy boots and pulled the top of the suit over his head. Fitting the metal ring of the pants into the ring of the shirt, he activated the seal around his waist.

"Computer, please record message." Chris pulled his

gloves and breather helmet out of the locker and clomped to the kitchen for a cup of water. "Mom? Dad? Please don't be mad, but I'm going topside for a meeting with this guy I met. I know what you're thinking, but he's legit. I'm sure he is. I know this is going to sound weird, but God wants me to go. Know how the Bible says we're supposed to reach out to people? Well, I decided I was going to try it this morning, and there this guy was. His mom's in quarantine, and he's all alone. He hasn't been person to person in months."

Chris pulled out a bottle of pills and swallowed one with a gulp of water. "His name is MarsColony3009, and the coordinates of his bunker are on the computer. I just swallowed a locator chip, so you shouldn't have any trouble finding me. Just in case, I'll dial in to a tracking satellite and have it monitor my progress." He pulled on his gloves and sealed them around his wrists. "Okay, here goes. I'll be back in an hour."

Checking the suit's air supply, he lowered the helmet over his head. The pounding of his heart echoed in his ears as he activated the neck seal. *Topside.* He couldn't believe he was really doing it. Radiation from the sun, microorganisms, wild creatures . . . He'd be in a completely uncontrolled environment. Anything could happen. He could be killed.

He carefully made his way through the kitchen, amazed at how alien everything looked through the gold-tinted visor of his helmet. Something bumped the side of his hip, and he stopped. The padded corner of the kitchen table. He felt his hip to make sure his suit wasn't damaged. So far so good. He moved carefully around the table and stepped onto the elevator platform.

Activating the lift with a command sequence from his

The Science behind the Story

Take Care of that Troposphere!

Think for a minute what life on Earth would be like without our atmosphere. What do we have to lose? Plenty! God has put our atmosphere around us as a protective shield, and it's over 348 miles deep. That seems like a lot, but it's the only thing between us and the freezing reaches of space. It also helps block the scorching radiation of the sun and recycle moisture.

But the atmosphere isn't the same everywhere. It's a little bit like a layer cake. The part we live in, the troposphere, reaches up nearly ten miles. Up there, winds howl and temperatures drop to -70° F. Brr.

Above the troposphere lies the next layer, the stratosphere. In the lower reaches, it's just plain chilly. But because of an important layer called ozone, the upper stratosphere (up to about 25 miles) can warm up to 65° F!

Warm to cold, then warm again, then . . . you guessed it. The third layer, the mesosphere, stretches 25 to 50 miles above the surface. In the upper reaches, temperatures drop down to -225° F, which is a little colder than Minnesota in January.

Then above 50 miles, the sun's radiation charges the air to a whopping 3600° F! These charged layers are called the ionosphere. Sometimes charged atoms can cause a green glow called auroras (the northern and southern lights) that form fantastic light shows.

So those are the four main layers. They're all important, and they're all specially designed for us down on the surface. But the fair-skinned among us still need to wear sunscreen on sunny days.

wrist controller, he braced himself against encircling rails as the platform rose toward the surface.

Almost there . . . he stepped into the airlock and sealed the hatch behind him. It took him several minutes to figure out how to work the controls, but he finally managed to evacuate the chamber and bring it up to exterior pressure.

A green button flashed next to the outer hatch. Taking a deep breath, he pressed the button and the heavy door swung open with a muffled hiss. Blinding yellow light pressed in on him, swirling all around him. It was too bright. He couldn't breathe.

Chris staggered forward, shielding his eyes with upraised arms. His heart pounded in his ears. He felt dizzy. If he fell . . . If a sharp object punctured his encounter suit . . . He looked down at the ground and squinted into the glare. Jagged rocks stabbed up all around him. Strange green plants . . . He picked his way through them, careful not to let them scrape his suit. He could do this. He couldn't go back now.

Chris punched Joel's coordinates into his controller and turned to his left, following the indicator on the directional display. The rocks were smaller here. Less jagged.

Suddenly an invisible force hit him in the chest, pushing him backward. Faint ticks and clicks sounded in his helmet. Brown projectiles flew past him. They were all around him, tumbling through the air like heat-seeking missiles.

He stumbled backward, windmilling his arms to keep his balance. Something snagged his foot and toppled him over. There were no force lines to catch him. No airbags popped out of the floor. He hit the ground with a resounding smack.

Pain surged through him, overloading his senses. His

skin felt wet. Clammy. A drop of moisture streaked down his face, burning his eyes. His suit was leaking; it had to be. He scrambled to his feet and checked the suit monitor. It didn't show any leaks, but it could have been damaged by the fall. It was too much. He had to go back. This was his life he was talking about—not some hologame.

He took a half step toward his bunker and froze.

A dark shadow was moving toward him. Rippling muscles. Jet black fur. Needle-sharp fangs . . .

He turned and fled, running blindly in the opposite direction. The rocky terrain rushed by him, a blur of browns and greens. He glanced back over his shoulder and ran faster. It was still behind him. He wasn't going to make it. He couldn't escape.

A loose rock turned beneath his foot and sent him tumbling to the ground. The world spun around him. Somehow he was back on his feet again. Running. Running toward an above-ground airlock. He saw a face pressed to the glass in the inner hatch. A face with puffy, dark eyes.

"Joel!" Chris threw open the hatch and slammed it shut behind him. The hiss of rushing air sounded all around him, mingling with his own panting breath. He'd made it. He was safe.

The inner hatch swung open, and Joel pulled Chris inside onto an elevator platform. "I can't believe it!" His face was radiant. "I can't believe you actually did it!"

Chris pulled off his helmet and filled his lungs with the clean, filtered air. "I know! Did you see the cat? It didn't have a collar; I think it was wild."

Joel nodded. "I watched you the whole way."

"And the wind. It was almost a hurricane. Stuff was flying everywhere. I think it might have been leaves."

"Did they hit you? Are you hurt? I can't believe . . ." His

voice cracked, and a tear ran down his cheek. "Earth is so dangerous this time of year. The sun's UV radiation count is off the chart. I can't believe you risked going topside. Whoever heard of someone visiting his next-door neighbor? It's the nicest thing anyone's ever done for me."

The hub seemed more dim than when we had left it. Dad's voice crackled in my headset. "I've just about got this navigation system licked. You guys need to be ready to go soon."

"Okay," I said into the microphone. Talismort looked sad. "Maybe we could come back someday," I offered.

Talismort scratched his chin. He eyed the door. "You can't go just yet," he said. There was an urgency in his voice.

"We'd better head for the airlock," Amy said. "So when Dad gets there—"

The door on the opposite side of the room slammed shut. I heard the door behind me do the same.

"As I said, not just yet." Talismort was smiling, but there was a coldness about it, an emptiness.

"Hey, Talismort," I said, spreading my hands in a friendly way. "I love a good joke, but Dad's going to wonder."

Talismort said nothing. He simply stared at us with a thin, cool smile.

Amy started to pace. Her voice had the shrill tone of panic. She started waving her hands around. She reminded me of our aunt Angelica. Aunt Angie is Italian, and she says she can't talk without moving her hands. "You can't just keep us here like . . . like prisoners!"

Talismort glanced at the closed door as his answer. So

much for his Santa Claus appearance. Now there was something sinister about him.

I felt a freight train thundering through my chest. The room was suddenly as hot as Venus. I didn't know what to do. "What do you want from us?" I demanded.

"Simple," he said. He leaned back in his chair and put his hands behind his head. "Can't you guess?"

"I know," Amy said. I was amazed at how calm she had suddenly become. "You want a story from us, don't you?"

Talismort's eyes sparkled. "Call it your exit fee. Your ticket to freedom. It gets lonely here. I need something to take with me when you're gone."

Amy put her hands on her hips. "Well, Mr. Lock and Key, I've got a story, and it's true."

"The best kind, my dear, the best kind."

"It happened to my cousin, Erin. She sent me her story over the cosmonet. It's an amusing story."

Will the Real Alien Please Stand Up?

Michael Carroll

Bernie Johnson has been running the Rimshot Café since I was in kindergarten. He bought it from some guy who wanted to go back to Earth. The guy said he missed green. Spent most of his time in the little greenhouse domes next to the restaurant. He was so homesick that he never worked, and the restaurant almost went out of business. So Bernie bought the place at a steal. The seller was desperate. It's a great place to work, and now that I'm in middle school, I can wait tables in the summer and on holidays. Perfect for a little spare change. And you run into the most interesting people.

To have a restaurant that's going to really make it, according to Bernie, you have to have something special. "Erin," he says to me, "it's all about marketing. It's a perfect place for a view, but a view's not enough."

So even though the Rimshot Café is perched over the edge of the biggest canyon on Mars (not to mention the entire solar system), Bernie needed something extra to make it go. Bernie's secret weapon is the sundaes. These piles of ice-cream-and-fudge joy are miniature versions of Olympus Mons—"towering volcanoes of flavor" as Bernie's hologlow signs put it.

But on that last day of summer two years ago, I could tell right away that it wasn't the hot fudge sundaes that brought the strange visitor into the restaurant. There was something not quite right about the Man. His skin was an odd creamy color, almost like it was covered in makeup. And he looked around a lot, sort of like he was in a spy movie. He didn't even seem to be interested in the menu, but he finally looked at the screen.

"So, sweetie, what's good here?" he growled.

I hate it when people call me sweetie.

"It's all great," I said. "Really, I've eaten everything on the menu."

The Man sat up straighter. "Oh, really? Well, then . . . hmm . . ."

He was holding the menu up, but he was peeking around it toward the counter and Bernie. Usually, first timers and tourists are distracted here. After all, you can look right out the glass walls and watch the famous Valles Marineris canyonlands spreading away as far as you can see. The colors of the canyon walls change with the moving sun. And there are the hang gliders. Glider wings are about three times as big on Mars because of the thin air, and people just love sailing by the restaurant to get a rise out of the diners. Then there are the ships: the big luxury blimp cruisers moor just outside the café, dropping off tourists and taking on travelers.

With all that going on, people do get distracted, all right, but not this guy. His attention was focused inside. Not on the food but on something else. It was as if he had never seen a restaurant, or hot fudge sundaes, or . . . humans. He was studying us.

He adjusted his hat, which he really should have taken off in a restaurant. Was he hiding something? Maybe underneath was a row of spikes or a pair of antennas. He shrugged his shoulders as he spoke. Through his gray titanium shirt, I could tell he was as skinny as a bag of bones.

He looked up at me with watery eyes and said, "I'll have the number two, bacon well done, please."

"Number two." I nodded.

He put his hand on my arm. "Make sure the bacon is very, very well done," he said. "Crispy."

His hand felt like a skeleton's. There was no sparkle in his eye, no hint of a smile on his lips. Just that flat expression as if he were sleepwalking.

"Yessir," I said, leaving as quickly as I could.

When I brought the order to Bernie, he leaned through the window and said, "That guy bothering you?"

"Not really," I said. "But he's sure checking the place out. And he's very concerned that his bacon is well-done."

Bernie took the order chip. "Must be an alien."

A chill slithered down my spine and cuddled up in my stomach. "Wh—why do you say that?"

"Aliens never eat uncooked meat. Makes them grow extra eyeballs." Bernie grinned and smacked his gum at me. "You can't kid a kidder, kiddo. Now get to work!"

"Don't joke about aliens," I said. "It's not funny."

The fact is, the guy was giving me the creeps.

The Man was gone by the end of my shift, which was just fine with me. I packed up my things and got ready to go.

"Need a ride home, kid?" Bernie asked.

Bernie was like an uncle to me, like a brother to my dad. He gave me rides home all the time, and I took him up on it. It would be dark soon, and I hate walking home when it's snowing carbon dioxide.

On the ride home, Bernie talked about the old days on Mars, days before there were people. He liked to talk about the early robot landers and the first pioneers living in dome homes. I knew he would ask me the question he always asked, and he did.

"Ever seen the *Viking I* landing site? Beautiful. The little spacecraft is still there after a hundred years."

"Yep, we went on vacation there."

"Oh yeah, seems like you told me that," Bernie said. He always asked me the same thing, and I always told him about our vacation.

"We saw the *Spirit* rover back at the Smithsonian too," I added.

"Ya see? That's just what I'm talking about. Some museum wants to take the other *Viking* back to Earth, but I think they should leave it. They say it's getting all ruined by the weather, but I say, hogwash. Leave *Viking II* where it belongs."

"*Viking II*? Isn't that the one that disappeared?" I asked. "Dad said it was on the news."

"I seem to remember something about that," Bernie grumbled. "Nothing's sacred anymore. Tourists cart off all the historical artifacts. Old Russian landers. Ancient British rovers. It's a shame."

"Maybe they'll find it again," I said, trying to cheer him up. He changed the subject and asked me about my day. I told him about the Man. "I tell you, there was something not right about him."

"Like what?"

"His skin, for one thing. Kinda pasty."

"Like he'd been on a transport from Earth for a few months?"

"Well, yeah, maybe. Tourists do get that way sometimes . . ." *Or maybe*, I thought, *he was covering up his green skin with makeup.*

Bernie punched in the navo key and turned to me as the air car took over driving. "What else about our mysterious character?"

"He was really skinny too." As soon as I started to say it out loud, it sounded silly. I kept trying. "And he was distracted. He looked around the menu, and he looked right through me."

"What do you think he was looking at?"

I wasn't sure quite how to put it, so I just blurted it out. "He was acting like he'd never been in a restaurant before. Like he'd never seen people before."

I braced myself for one of Bernie's jokes, but it didn't come. Instead, he wore a serious expression. He was thinking about something.

The air car coasted to a stop on the roof of my house. "Wanna come in?" I asked.

"No time, Erin. Thanks anyway. Tell your dad and mom hi. When do you come in next?"

"Saturday lunch shift, I think."

"See ya then." He waved as I stepped out into the airlock. The door sealed. I watched through the porthole as Bernie's car banked toward the west and into the starry, purple twilight.

"And you know there's no such thing as aliens, right?"

That's my brother. Always the practical one. Peter is two years older than me. When I told him about the mysterious visitor, my own words sounded even sillier than when I had talked to Bernie.

"Yes, Peter, I know there's no such thing as aliens." I couldn't make my voice sound as certain as I wanted it to.

"Let's face it, Erin. People really don't come to the Rimshot for the sundaes. They come to see the big ditch. A canyon that big is enough to make anyone a little twitchy."

"I suppose you're right."

"Just try to keep it in mind the next time you go to work. The guy's not an alien. He's just some geeky computer jockey from Earth or something."

Somehow, I wasn't completely reassured. Peter could tell. He leaned forward and lowered his voice. "Tell ya what: next time he comes in, call me and I'll have a look. If I'm at home, I can be there in two minutes."

"Okay, you're on." I was half hoping he wouldn't get the chance.

I was wrong.

The café was dead, especially for a Saturday. The tourist cruiser from Earth hadn't sent down its shuttles yet, and there weren't many natives out. It was cold and windy out, and the sky was murky with spring dust.

Bernie was his normal, cheerful self. We joked around, and I took care of two or three tables. At about three o'clock, things got decidedly colder. The Man walked in and sat at a table on the far wall.

"There's our alien again," Bernie whispered. "You're on. But watch out for those death rays."

I hustled over to the table.

"Hi again," I said. The Man looked embarrassed that I remembered him. "Welcome to the Rimshot Café. May I hang up your hat?"

"Oh, no thank you. My head gets cold."

Yeah, right, I thought. But I said, "Can I get you something to drink?"

"I think I'll have water with lots of ice."

"Water," I nodded.

He said, "With lots and lots of—"

"Ice," I said.

"Yes. I'm used to things being colder than they are here," he said, looking down at the table. "Colder and darker."

I didn't ask. As I walked to the kitchen, I passed customers drinking espresso, coffee, hot tea, hot chocolate, but no one was drinking anything cold. It was that kind of day. But this guy, he was different.

"He won't take his hat off," I told Bernie.

"That's just high fashion. Anyway, the customer's always right. Go to it."

I stepped to the senso-bev dispenser. As the glass filled, I raised my wrist phone and spoke Peter's number.

"Yeah?"

"Peter, it's me. Where are you?"

"Home. Is he there?"

"Yes, and not so loud!" I whispered.

"Ooh, the alien's back. I'll be right over."

I brought the Man his drink. He held up the straw as

if it were a complete mystery to him. He glanced around and then unwrapped it. "How nice," he said. He put the straw gently into his glass, pulled it out and dipped it in again, then took a tentative sip through it. His eyes looked back and forth, scanning the restaurant.

He picked up his menu, then put it down again. "Say, may I ask you a question?" He looked into my eyes.

Did I feel something supernatural? Was I getting sleepy?

"Miss?" he said.

"Oh, er, yes. What is it?"

"The last time I was here, I had a wonderful salad. So fresh. How do they do that?"

So in addition to well-cooked bacon, the alien eats veggies, I thought. And he was hot on this cold day. Maybe he was from some cold place like Pluto. People had never been there yet. How would we know?

"How do they do what?" I asked.

"Get such fresh lettuce and tomatoes and cucumbers? Is there a greenhouse here?"

"Yep, there is," I said proudly. "This restaurant raises all its own fresh veggies in its own greenhouses."

A look of comprehension crossed his strange face. "Ah, so there's more than one?"

"Yep. One on the rise above the building and one just to the left."

"Don't know how I missed it," he mumbled.

Missed it? Was he looking for something? My mind raced. I remembered this old science fiction movie where an alien lands at a base in the arctic, and he plants pods in the greenhouse—pods that turn into other aliens!

"Missed what?" I said just a little too loudly.

"The second greenhouse." He thought for a moment. "Say, have you ever been inside these greenhouses?"

I was feeling suspicious. The fact is, I had been in the big one but Bernie never took me into the smaller one. He said it was just full of green beans and air-conditioning equipment.

"Once or twice," I said. It was only a half lie.

"Lots of pretty flowers?" He cocked his head the way a praying mantis does just before it eats its mate.

"Just vegetables."

"Well, then never mind that. I've made up my mind. I'd just love one of those famous Rimshot hot fudge sundaes. They don't have hot fudge where I come from."

No hot fudge? That left out Earth as his home sweet home. And if he wasn't from Earth, where could he be from? I wanted to ask him, but the words stuck in my throat. I felt hot all over.

"One hot fudge, coming right up," I croaked.

I forgot to ask if he wanted nuts. I forgot to ask if he wanted chocolate ice cream or vanilla or strawberry or all three, or even bananas or a cherry. I just stumbled to the counter with his order. In the end, Bernie gave him the works, and he seemed pleased.

Peter was nowhere to be seen. Where could he be? The Man gestured to me. I slowly went to his table.

"Miss, may I have the bill?"

"Sure thing, coming right up."

I made my way to the counter, stalling as long as I could. I looked at the entrance. No Peter. I punched in the table code, and the computer spit out the bill. I turned just in time to see my brother walking through the doorway.

I stepped to the table dramatically so as to get Peter's attention, but he made a beeline to the counter. He and Bernie began some deep discussion about Martian soccer or something. I handed the peculiar patron his bill, then ran back to the counter.

"Do you see, Peter?" I jabbed a finger in his chest. "That's him. Watch!"

The Man shoved his credit card into the table slot, pulled it out, and left quietly. He didn't really walk out the door. He sort of slid, as if he was fighting the floor. Gravity. What a concept.

"Yes," Peter said seriously. "No human could have paid for his lunch like that!"

I punched him in the shoulder.

"So he walks funny and keeps his hat on," Peter said, but his eyes were still on the door, and there was uncertainty in his voice.

"You gotta admit, he's—"

"Weird." Peter finished my sentence. "I'm going home, sis."

The Man's questions haunted me. What could be so interesting about a greenhouse? Was there something hidden in there that an alien would want?

At the end of my shift, Rose came in to take over. She's my favorite waitress. Charlie, the chef, came in at about the same time. The restaurant was covered. Now was my chance. I asked Bernie if we could go see the small greenhouse. He gave me the it's-all-beans-and-equipment line, but I persisted.

"I've never been in there in all the years I've worked here," I whined.

"I suppose it wouldn't hurt," he said. "Charlie, you and Rose hold down the fort for a while." Bernie turned to me. "Before we go back there, I want to show you something I keep in the office."

"Sure."

Bernie led me back to his cramped office. His desk was piled with papers and forms and cookbooks, as usual. He pointed to a little plaque hanging crooked on the wall. It said,

The Science behind the Story

Valleys and Vikings

Valles Marineris is a big crack that opened up when the largest volcanoes in the solar system erupted. It's five times as deep as Arizona's Grand Canyon. If it were on Earth, it would stretch from Los Angeles to Boston—so long that part of it is in night while part of it is in daylight. The change in air temperature from one end to the other sets up supersonic winds in the chasm.

The canyon's name means "valleys of *Mariner.*" The *Mariner 9* spacecraft first found it in 1971. The *Mariner* spacecraft paved the way for the first successful landers on Mars, the *Viking I* and *Viking II*. On July 20, 1976, the Volkswagen-size *Viking I* landed on Chryse Planitia, the "plains of gold." *Viking II* also landed safely. Both landers beamed back daily weather reports, searched for life with onboard biology laboratories, and scanned the landscape and sky. The *Viking* landers had tiny nuclear power plants. *Viking II* lasted for about five years!

There have been other landings on Mars since. The most recent attempts were made in December 2003 and January 2004. The Mars rover *Spirit*, launched by NASA, landed inside the Connecticut-size Gusev Crater. A second NASA rover, *Opportunity*, landed in a shallow crater in an area called Meridiani Planum. As of this writing, the rovers continue to drive great distances studying this frigid and beautiful desert world.

Scientists are studying plans for more rovers, landers, gliders, and balloons to visit Mars. In the near future, engineers plan to send a robot that would bring back some rock and soil samples for study here on Earth, with the ultimate dream of one day sending people. Maybe you will be one of the first to go!

God does not judge by external appearance.

Galatians 2:6

Bernie pointed a wrinkled finger at the sign. "You know why I have that there? It's to remind me that no matter who walks in that door, no matter what they look like or how they talk or what they wear, they are important to God. And it's important to God that I treat them that way."

Bernie didn't lecture. He suggested. But this was a strong suggestion. I got the picture. *I suppose God even loves aliens*, I thought to myself. *But Bernie doesn't know the truth about this guy, and what he doesn't know might be very, very bad for him.*

We went down the hall, through a double airlock, and into the fresh-smelling, heavy air of the greenhouse. Bernie led us to the opposite side and through a small door. It opened into a place I'd never been: the second greenhouse. It was smaller than the first, and it lacked the big trees and brightly colored fruit. Here were rows of low plants, mostly carrots, lettuce, and beans.

Bernie swept his hand before him. "Welcome to my second greenhouse. See? I told you. Lots of beans."

"Can I explore?" I asked.

"Be my guest."

I wandered around for a little while. I love the smell of moist dirt and wet leaves. You don't get to smell that kind of thing very often on Mars. As I moved toward the back of the building, Bernie called. "'Bout time to go, kiddo."

As I turned to leave, I saw a bunch of gray pipes sticking up from behind some plants. "Hey, what's back here?" I called.

"Nothing. Just some air-conditioning equipment and stuff."

The pipes were sticking out of a grayish box that looked

very old. It was about the size of a small car. It looked familiar.

"Let's go, Erin. It's getting late."

We left, but I knew I'd seen that contraption somewhere before.

The next time I went to work, I could tell something was up. Charlie was working the counter, and Rose looked like she was waiting for a meteor to fall on the place. I put on my name tag—Bernie insists we wear name tags—and went to Rose.

"What's going on?"

Rose's eyebrows wandered up and down her forehead. "You know that weird guy who's been coming in?"

I slapped my hands together. "I just knew it was something about him!"

"Well, hang on tight, sister. He comes in here, and he asks for Bernie by name. He says, 'Is Mr. Bernie Johnson present?' and I says, 'I'll check,' and he says, 'Thank you so much,' but kinda like a cold fish. So Bernie comes out, and they chat and then disappear."

"They disappeared? Like in some kind of cosmic transporter?"

"No, no, they just walked out the back door. Toward the—"

"Greenhouses!" I ran down the hallway with a spatula in my hand. Bernie might be in mortal danger! I burst through the first greenhouse. No one was there. They must have been in the second one. I opened the door a crack. I could hear Bernie's voice. He was very quiet.

"You can't have it."

"Even for seven thousand?" the Man was saying.

"It's not the money. It's a piece of history, and nobody should take it away."

I leaned through the door just far enough to see what was going on.

"But it landed so far north that the poor thing is falling apart." The Man's voice was soft, maybe even a little kind.

"It belongs here," Bernie said.

The Man shrugged. He took his hat off. Underneath was not a row of spikes or a pair of antennas. There was just a bald head with a wisp of gray hair on the very top.

"I'm sorry you feel that way," the Man said.

"Are you going to turn me in?"

The strange visitor smiled. "I wouldn't dream of it. We hope that one day you'll change your mind."

The two men stood up, and Bernie shook the Man's hand. I couldn't believe it. This Man, this thing, was threatening my boss, and he was shaking hands with him? With *it*? Bernie must have been under some kind of spell. There was nothing left to do. I ran in swinging my spatula. Unfortunately, it wasn't very effective, being soft plastic. But my wild screaming got their attention.

"AARRGH!" I yelled.

Bernie leaped forward and grabbed the spatula. "Erin, what are you doing?"

"I've come to save you!"

"No need." Bernie was smiling, and for the first time, so was the Man.

Bernie turned to him. "Mr. Clarence, I want you to meet my best employee, Erin."

The Man stuck out his hand. "We've met. But not officially."

"Who, wha . . . what . . . how come . . ." I said.

"Mr. Clarence is from an office on the asteroid Eros. It's the main office of the Marsden Museum."

I'd heard of the place. The Marsden Museum was the biggest museum on Earth, with offices on the moon, Mars, Eros, and one of Jupiter's moons. It made sense that the Man lived on an asteroid. No wonder he had a hard time walking around on Mars, which had ten times the gravity of his home world.

I put my hands on my hips and looked at Bernie. "Does this have something to do with that air-conditioning system back there?"

Bernie spread his hands. "It's not really an air conditioner. It's, ah, something more important."

Mr. Clarence piped in. "In fact, young lady, it's the *Viking II* lander. Came from Earth in 1976. Do you know your history?"

"I'm not so hot on the Renaissance, but I know that part. *Viking II*, isn't that the one that was stolen?"

Weirdly enough, the alien-looking museum guy came to Bernie's defense. "Stolen is a strong word. Your friend was trying to keep the lander here on Mars."

"Because," Bernie interjected, "it's part of Martian history. But the museum wants to take it back to Earth and put it on display. I was going to put it back at its landing site as soon as they lost interest."

"And you," I said, pointing to Mr. Clarence, aka the Man, "wanted to take it from Bernie?"

"Actually," Bernie said, "Mr. Clarence was trying to help. He didn't want the police involved. He just wanted to give me a chance to give it to the museum."

"Why?" I asked.

Mr. Clarence perked up as if he was about to give a lecture. I hoped I was wrong. "Good question. Until Bernie took it, *Viking II* wasn't holding up as well as its sister craft, *Viking I*. *Viking II* landed farther north, and the cold was cracking it. Sand was getting inside. Our archaeologists are afraid there won't be anything left soon."

"Why can't you put it back at its landing site and cover it up somehow, put a glass dome over it?"

"Too late. The poor thing is just crumbling away. It needs to be fixed."

I got an idea. Maybe it was a crazy idea, but maybe it would work. I leaned over and whispered in Bernie's ear. When I stood up straight, he was grinning.

Bernie said to Mr. Clarence, "Could you refurbish it in this greenhouse and then put it back where it belongs with a dome over it?"

The Man put his hand to his pointed little chin. "Hmm . . ."

"I'd serve the museum staff free lunch for as long as they were here, and you could open a museum visitor center right at the site."

"Well, I'll have to make some calls, but it sounds good to me. Little lady, you have a good head on your shoulders!"

Just then I imagined the Man with spikes going down his bald head and two little antennas sticking out. "So do you," I said. And I meant it. This guy, this strange man who I thought was an alien, turned out to be a kind friend to Bernie.

I still had one question. "Hey, Bernie, where can I buy a sign like the one in your office?"

"I'll get you one. It's a good reminder."

"Reminder of what?" the Man asked.

I said, "Just a reminder that you can't judge people by what they look like on the outside."

"It's a good thing," Mr. Clarence said. "I'd hate to know what people would think of little old me!"

Talismort clapped. "That's a lovely story, Amy. And now, Jason, it's your turn."

I'm not the greatest storyteller. I know a few jokes, but when I'm nervous I can't remember anything, let alone some tale Talismort would be interested in. And I was nervous. I thought about running across the room and trying the door. What would he ask next? Would one story be enough? If I got really scared, I could always call Dad on the headset, but sometimes he took his headset off when he was working. What would Talismort do if I tried to call for help and no one was there?

Talismort seemed to read my mind. "You could run out the airlock. But then you wouldn't stay awake very long in the vacuum of space."

"Eleven seconds," I mumbled.

"What was that?" Talismort asked.

"Eleven seconds. That's how long you can stay awake in a vacuum. I know of three people who learned the hard way. A guy named Brandon, a very foxy girl named Megan, and a really special young man named Josh."

········ **14** ········

Eleven Seconds

Randall Ingermanson

Hide-and-seek is a kid's game, so I normally wouldn't have been playing it at all yesterday. When you're thirteen years old, the last thing in the world you want is to play a kid's game.

Except that Megan was playing.

Megan McDaniel is . . . how shall I say this? . . . Special. Megan has soft blond hair that hangs to her waist and eyes as blue as the sky back on Earth. But that's not why she's special.

Megan was the second baby born on Mars.

I was first, but I guess everybody already knows that. When I was born, the news geeks on Earth made a big deal out of it. Brandon Allen, first baby on Mars, woohoo. Two months later, Megan came along, and by that time it was big whoop. That's just how newspeople are. First is the only thing that matters to them. Second doesn't count.

The truth is, first hasn't been such a great deal either. By the time Megan and I were three, the doctors realized something was wrong with us. Mars has a lot lower gravity than Earth, which means Megan and I have grown up our whole lives in a different environment than humans were designed for. We're taller than normal. Skinnier. Our internal bone structure isn't as strong as it should be. Our spines have the wrong curvature. Nowadays, kids born on Mars spend months in a centrifuge to simulate higher gravity, and that seems to help.

But it's too late for Megan and me. We're freaks, sort of. We'll never be right. So I watch out for her, and she looks out for me.

Yesterday Megan wanted to play hide-and-seek with the younger kids. The normal kids. I would rather have been reading, but she really wanted to play, and I really wanted to keep an eye on her—both of which turned out to be very bad ideas.

Josh Ryder was "it." Josh is ten years old and was born on Earth, and everybody hates him. I double hate him because he's three years younger than I am and he's already a lot stronger, which isn't fair. I am what I am because of where I was born, not because of anything I did.

But there's another reason I hate Josh. His family is religious, which is illegal on Mars. I don't get why they came here in the first place. Mars is off-limits to religion. We're building a new world, and we don't want any of Earth's problems. My dad says religion is just another word for trouble. The colony is going to send the Ryders back to Earth on the next launch opportunity, but that won't be for another year. Meanwhile, Josh always has this smug little smile on his geeky face, and I triple hate him for that.

Anyway, Josh started counting, and all the kids scattered. The twenty-four habitation modules at Base Camp One are linked together in one big ring. I know a perfect hiding place in hab fourteen. The whole lower floor of that hab is a metal shop with all kinds of cool stuff—lathes and a drill press and lots of tools in a big cabinet.

When I got to hab fourteen, I heard giggling. I yanked open the door of the tool cabinet and found the Wilmington twins in there. Jessica and Ashley, five years old. The two of them had my hiding place all locked up.

"Shh, don't tell!" one of them said.

I shut the cabinet and ran out. Away down the corridor, I heard Josh hollering, "Ready or not, here I come!"

Great. I was going to get caught again. By a religious geek. I turned and ran the other way. There was no way I'd give Josh the satisfaction of catching me.

Hab fifteen is a child-care center—just a big open space with lots of toys and little kids and nowhere to hide. I ran through.

Hab sixteen is a library with a bunch of computers for reading. Useless for hiding.

Hab seventeen is a locker area. There's an airlock to go outside. There are about fifty lockers, each containing an EVA suit.

And there's a second airlock to go into the greenhouse. The greenhouse is an inflatable pressurized dome, but it's off-limits unless you're wearing an EVA suit. Once every couple of years, a meteorite punctures the greenhouse and the whole thing explosively decompresses. Martian ambient pressure is about 1 percent of normal pressure. My folks have told me five million times how long a person can last in Martian ambient pressure.

Eleven seconds.

After that, you pass out. A minute later, you die.

They don't make EVA suits for kids, so I've never been in the greenhouse.

About two habs behind me, I heard Josh hollering something. I jumped in one of the lockers and left the door hanging all the way open. I figured it looked less suspicious that way.

Josh's footsteps thumped into the locker room. I heard the clatter of a locker door being yanked open.

"Caught ya!" Josh hollered.

I heard a disappointed sigh. I'd know that sigh anywhere. "Josh, it's not fair," Megan said. "I can't run fast. You've got to give me another chance."

A long pause. "Sure, Meg."

I hate it when Josh calls her Meg. It makes it sound like she's special to him. Which she isn't. Not at all.

"Go around the whole ring once," Megan said. "That'll give me a fair chance to find a good hiding place."

Silence for a few seconds. "Okay, that sounds fair, Meg."

Footsteps raced out of the locker room.

I climbed out of my locker. "Hi, Megan."

Megan's face looked soft and pink. "Oh! I didn't know you were here too!"

"Let's hide somewhere. The little geek'll be back in a few minutes."

"Will you hide with me?" Megan gave me a smile that twisted my stomach into a tight little knot.

"Um . . . sure. Where do you want to hide?"

"There." Megan pointed at the greenhouse. She grabbed my hand. "Come on. I'm sick of Josh always catching me. He'll never think to look in there."

"Megan, it's not . . . safe in the greenhouse."

Megan pulled me along. "We'll just hide in the airlock."

I didn't think that was such a great hiding place—the airlock's got a window. But Megan is a pretty determined girl when she gets an idea in her head. And besides, her hand felt very warm and . . . nice. My heart started whumping in my chest so loud I thought sure Megan would notice.

We crammed inside the airlock and pulled the door shut. It was tight in there, just big enough for one adult in an EVA suit. Barely big enough for the two of us. We tried to crouch down below the level of the window, but it didn't work. Megan and I are both tall. We couldn't crouch low enough.

"Phooey!" Megan finally said. "This isn't working." She pushed open the outer door of the airlock. "Come on. We'll go just a little way into the greenhouse."

"Megan . . ."

"What?" A big pout formed on her lips.

"You know. Eleven seconds and all that."

Megan pulled me down the three steps into the greenhouse. "We're right here by the airlock. Look, I'm leaving the outer door open. If anything happens, we'll jump back inside. It won't take more than a second. Besides, the chances are about one in a million."

She had a point. And anyway, she was still holding my hand. I liked that. I liked it a lot.

The greenhouse had a rich, ripe, green smell. The colony has about twenty greenhouses scattered around the hab ring, and we grow all our food in them. Mars doesn't have soil; it has regolith, which is basically rock crushed up into a fine dust. Soil would have organic stuff—dead plants and bugs and worms and whatever. Plants grow fine in regolith, but they need water and nutrients. The whole greenhouse has this amazing drip-irrigation system my dad designed. He's told me all about it, but until yesterday, I'd never actually seen it.

"Look at that!" Megan pointed at a long row of flower beds off on the right side. "Those are beautiful."

They were incredibly beautiful. My dad's been experimenting with roses lately. He keeps hoping to breed a blue rose, which is supposedly impossible. It's a hobby of his. The best he's done is a light violet, which is still pretty cool.

Megan's eyes were shining now. "Do you think it would be okay if I . . . picked one?"

"Sure. My dad wouldn't miss it."

Megan plucked a rose and inhaled deeply. "Oh, that smells so good. Smell it."

I took a sniff. If you ask me, a rose's smell isn't such a big deal. But girls think different.

"Smells nice," I said.

Megan gave me a shy smile. My heart did a double back-flip. She'd never looked at me like that before. She pulled off a petal and handed it to me. "He loves me." Another petal. "He loves me not." Another one. "He loves me."

My chest felt like I had a piece of molten lead sitting where my heart should be.

Megan kept pulling off petals and handing them to me. Finally only two were left. "He loves me not . . . He loves me." She gave me the last two petals and looked deep into my eyes.

My head felt like it was full of helium. I couldn't say a word, my mouth was so dry.

Megan leaned closer to me. "Well?"

I was so scared, I wanted to run. "Well what?" I rasped.

"Does he love me or doesn't he?"

I couldn't breathe. "Does who?"

She wrapped her hands around my waist. "You."

"I . . ." Panic wrapped a fist around my heart. "Um, yeah."

Megan tilted her head up and pressed her lips against mine. For a moment, I felt like I was flying. Her lips were as soft and warm as a bazillion roses. I kissed her. It was better than I ever—

Boom!

For a second, I didn't know what had happened. Then I heard the decompression alarm. The roar of rushing air filled the greenhouse. Megan and I pulled apart.

"Run!" I shouted.

We were only twenty yards from the airlock door. We had plenty of time. I was dead sure we could make it back in time.

Except that Megan tripped right in front of me and fell across a planter box.

I fell on top of her. I heard the sound of bone cracking. Not my bone. Hers.

By the time I got on my feet again, I was gasping for breath. The air was so thin, I could barely hear the sound of the decompression alarm.

Megan was on the ground, clutching her leg. "Go!" she shouted. "Get help!"

I knew there wasn't time. Nobody could help Megan except me. I grabbed her around the waist and hefted her up. Megan screamed. I was hurting her, but there was no other way. I was hyperventilating now, breathing as fast as I could, and it wasn't enough. I staggered toward the airlock. My chest hurt, and my brain felt like it was turning to mush. I heard a faint pounding sound and looked up at the airlock.

Josh was beating on the window of the inner door with both hands, shouting something. But he couldn't open the door, because we'd left the outer one open.

Somehow, I dragged Megan to the bottom step of the airlock. My lungs were on fire, and my legs felt like wood. I tried to step up.

My feet wouldn't lift. I wanted desperately to just fall forward into the lock, to collapse on its floor. But two people couldn't lie in that tiny space. It was me or Megan.

I spun around and heaved Megan into the airlock. I lost my balance. Fell to my knees. Shoved Megan's legs up into the airlock. Slammed the door behind her.

Somewhere in the back of my brain, I knew my eleven seconds were up.

The world went black.

"Please, Brandon, wake up." It was my mom's voice, sounding really close and really far away at the same time. My skin was on fire, and my lungs felt like they were full of battery acid.

I cracked my eyes open. My parents were staring down at me. I could see the white walls of the hospital hab. Somehow, I had survived.

"He's awake!" My mom sagged to her knees and started crying.

Which was kind of dumb, because it was me who was hurting, not her, but mothers are like that.

My dad leaned down close, looking solemn. "Brandon, can you hear us?"

My heart gave a funny lurch in my chest. His face had a look like I'd died. I gave a little nod, which was about all I could do. "Yeah," I whispered. "I hear you."

"Brandon!" A blond head leaned into view. "Brandon, you're alive!" Megan looked like she'd been crying.

I coughed. "I'm alive."

All of a sudden, I realized that it didn't make sense. I'd used up my eleven seconds saving Megan. I should be dead. Only I wasn't.

"Megan!" I whispered. My throat felt raw. "What . . . happened?"

My mother backed up, and Megan hobbled closer on crutches. Tears were burning down her cheeks, and her lips looked soft and red.

Megan heaved a big sigh. "As soon as you shut the airlock, Josh pumped it up to pressure and pulled me into the locker room."

Something cold filled up my chest. Josh? That grinning little geek helped save Megan? It wasn't fair. Now he would be strutting around Base Camp One letting everyone pat him on the back and make a big deal about what a hero he was. From now on, I was going to quadruple hate the little creep.

Except that I still didn't get why I was alive. I licked my lips. "Megan . . . how did I . . . ?"

All of a sudden, everybody got real quiet. My mom covered her face in her hands. My dad got that solemn look on his face again. Megan bit her lip.

"What's going on?" I hissed through clenched teeth. This wasn't making sense at all.

"He needs to know," my dad said.

Mom sighed and dabbed at her face with a fistful of tissues.

Tears started pouring down Megan's face. "Brandon . . . Josh went into the airlock and . . . pumped it down to vacuum and . . . saved you too."

I felt sick all the way to my bones. Josh had saved my life. The little jerk would be insufferable from now on. I'd never be able to look at his grinning face again. This was horrible beyond words. Quintuple hate.

The Science behind the Story

No Pressure, Man!

Arnold Schwarzenegger steps out into the Martian wilderness in the movie *Total Recall*. He gazes into the eyes of a beautiful woman and then pitches off a cliff, breaking the faceplate of his helmet against a rock. His suit decompresses as air streams from his helmet. His face swells up, his tongue sticks out, and his eyeballs explode. Not a pretty picture.

What would really happen to a person in a vacuum? Medical studies suggest that Arnold's death wouldn't have been nearly so dramatic. While your eardrums might burst, they would heal (if you were rescued in time), and your eyeballs, at least for a minute or so, would probably be fine. The real problem is that you would have only about eleven seconds to save yourself. After that, you would lose consciousness.

What about your lungs? In the classic movie *2001: A Space Odyssey*, astronaut Dave Bowman must blow himself into the vacuum of space through an open door, close the door, and fill the room with air before he conks out. Could he? Maybe. But Bowman made a serious mistake: he held his breath. As any deep-sea diver knows, you must let the air out of your lungs as pressure drops, or they might rupture. In addition, your body will swell up as water inside tries to get outside, but these effects will go away if your exposure lasts less than a couple of minutes. The more time you spend in a vacuum, the more damage is done to your bod, and seconds count.

So the best thing to do in a vacuum is let the air out of your lungs, blink your eyes a lot so they don't freeze, and *don't panic*! You still have eleven seconds to get yourself out!

Megan was bawling her eyes out. I didn't get it. She could see I was safe, couldn't she? Yeah, I'd be in the hospital for a few days, but I wasn't going to die or anything. I was going to get better. Everything was going to be fine.

Finally Megan got control of herself. She smeared her eyes with the back of her hand and sniffed hard. "Brandon . . . Josh saved you, but . . . he couldn't get back in the airlock himself."

It hit me like a hammer in the head. Josh had died in my place.

The guy I hated more than anyone in the whole world had died for me.

"Oh," I said. It must have sounded cold, but I couldn't think right then.

Something hot was filling up the whole inside of my chest. All of a sudden, I couldn't see very well.

Megan clutched my hand. "I love you, Brandon."

I wanted to say something, wanted to tell her I loved her, but not with my mom and dad standing right there. Megan's really special to me. So special that I'd . . . you know. Die for her. That's what you do for people you care about. For people who love you.

But you don't do that for people who hate you.

I saved Megan because I love her.

What I don't get is why Josh saved me. I've always hated him. He's always known it.

And he died for me anyway.

I don't get that. I don't get it at all.

Talismort smiled. "That was excellent. You're both turning out to be wonderful storytellers."

"Thanks," I said flatly.

"Oh, now, don't be grumpy at my little trick. Try the door. It was never locked."

I did. It swung open freely.

"I hope you'll forgive an old man for a little drama. Shall we go?"

Somehow, I couldn't stay mad at the ancient storyteller and his little pranks. His eyes were kind, and he had spent so much time with us, sharing hot chocolate and adventures. A story or two from us wasn't much to ask.

Talismort led us to the door, trailed by a scattering of pearl lights. He reached into his pocket and pulled out a polished, yellowish rock. He placed it carefully in an empty stand on the shelf next to the Mars rocks.

"My newest piece for the collection. Even your father is a good spinner of tales. He told me about your adventure at the golden asteroid, and he gave me a piece of it. Another story to add to my anthology. Very nice."

Something clanged against the hatch on the far wall.

"Now what?" Amy said.

We opened the hatch, and there, with his arms full of equipment, tools, and energy transformers, stood Dad.

"Oh dear," Talismort said. "You've brought supplies."

"I'm actually cleaning up. All done. I told you I'd have your communications up and running in no time."

Amy tugged at Talismort's sleeve. "Now you'll be able to tell your stories to lots of people!"

"Stories, yes. That would be so nice. There's power in stories, you know. The good defeating evil in *Star Wars*, the triumph over temptation in The Lord of the Rings, the deep lessons of *Moby Dick* and *David Copperfield* and The Chronicles of Narnia."

We nodded, encouraging him on.

"To be sure, there are lessons to be learned even from fairy tales. But think of the stories from the Bible, every one true to the last detail. Think how those have changed the world. Changed history. Changed people. Yes, stories are important. And now, thanks to your rescue of my battered little space station, I can continue my adventures," Talismort said, wagging a finger at us.

"Maybe you could even write a book," I suggested.

"A book, yes," he said, holding his chin and looking at the ceiling. "People do love to read. A book about all the adventures of this high frontier, all the stories we find just over the horizon we are so used to. Maybe in a Martian setting. I could call it . . . *Martian Dust* . . . or . . ."

We said our good-byes and thanked Talismort. Dad wished him good sailing in the dark seas of space. As we closed the last hatch, I wondered what new adventures would meet him, and if we would ever hear those stories.

Amy leaned over to me and whispered, "I do hope he writes a book. But I think the title needs a little work!"

Dad held up his hand. "I think I forgot my C7 generator! Let's see if we can find it quick."

We turned back into the station. Talismort looked surprised to see us. "Welcome to my little space station!" he cried.

"I forgot one of my tools," Dad said. "It's about the size of your hand, black with a red handle. It can be in only a couple of places. Kids, you look in here, and I'll go down to engineering."

Dad disappeared through a hatch, and we looked around the hub. Talismort seemed a little confused. Then, a look of recognition passed across his face. "Ah, the asteroid surveyors," he said.

It was our turn to be confused. "You act as if you haven't seen us in a while," Amy said.

He pointed to his temple. "This old brain, you know. Would either of you like some hot chocolate?"

"That might be nice." Dad's voice came from behind. We hadn't heard him come back in.

"Did you find it?" I asked him.

Dad didn't seem to hear. He said, "And maybe a short story?"

That was just weird. One minute Dad was in a hurry to get back to the ship, and the next he wanted a bedtime story?

My headset crackled. It was Dad's voice. "Hey, guys, I've got it. Meet you at the airlock." Where was that voice coming from? And who was this standing in front of us? Suddenly, Dad's body wavered, the way the roadway does on a summer afternoon. He vanished. Talismort smiled.

The lights flickered. "Looks like we need to give our

power cells a rest," he said, looking up at the lights. "All this excitement."

The lights dimmed again, and this time, so did Talismort.

He looked at us with those wise eyes and gentle grin. "You see, a perfectly interactive program. I learn from you, and—hopefully—you learn a few things from me."

"But . . . but . . ." Amy said. "But I felt your sleeve!" She reached over and touched Talismort's long hand.

I pointed to the tiny lights along the ceiling. "May I?" I asked.

He nodded.

I climbed up on to the counter and put my hand over one of the pearl lights. The left side of his body turned to mist, like a holovideo that isn't working quite right. "Now try it."

Amy reached for Talismort's sleeve. Her hand went right through it.

"You see," our phantom friend said, "my ship is the perfect storyteller. And now that you have visited, I have even more wonderful things to share with other visitors." The lights flickered again, and we could see through Talismort, right to the chair beneath him. "It's time for you to go and me to rest. Your father is waiting."

I was just a little creeped out. I grabbed Amy by the hand and pulled her toward the airlock. Her hand was warm and real, and it felt reassuring.

She called over her shoulder, "Thanks, Talismort!"

"Thank you, kids. Come again!"

And I thought that someday we just might.

About the Contributors

Sigmund Brouwer is an award-winning novelist and children's book author with more than two million books sold. He is co-founder of the Young Writers Institute. His articles on helping children read and write have appeared in *Focus on the Family* magazine. Over the last ten years, he has spoken to over 250,000 students at schools across the United States and Canada, ranging from schools north of the Arctic Circle to inner-city Los Angeles. His latest novel, *The Last Disciple*, is cowritten with Hank Hanegraaff and part of a trilogy that deals with end times.

Michael Carroll's *Exploring Ancient Cities of the Bible* spawned trivia games and websites when introduced five years ago. When he's not painting planets or dinosaurs, Carroll writes science articles for magazines like *Popular Science*, *Clubhouse*, and *Odyssey*. His work has also been featured on *NOVA*, *COSMOS*, and various other TV specials for Public Television. Along with his coauthor wife, he has also written more than a dozen books for young readers and teens about science and faith, including *Dinosaurs*. He lives in Littleton, Colorado, with his wife, two fine teens, and a few seahorses.

Jim Denney has been a full-time writer since 1989 and has produced nearly sixty books. His most recently published books are the four books in the Timebenders science fiction series for young readers, beginning with *Battle Before Time*. Jim's most recent nonfiction book, *Answers to Satisfy the Soul*, examines twenty of life's most perplexing questions, from "How can I find happiness?" to "Does God exist?" Jim currently lives on the West Coast with his wife and two kids. Visit his website at www .denneybooks.com/Timebenders.html.

Marianne Dyson has a degree in physics and was one of the first women NASA flight controllers. She won the 2000 Golden Kite Award for *Space Station Science* and the 2004 American Institute of Physics Science Writing Award for *Home on the Moon*. Her other work includes *The Space Explorer's Guide to Stars and Galaxies* (Scholastic's Space University series) and short fiction in *Analog*, *Breakaway*, *Child for Life*, and *Best of Girls to the Rescue*. A frequent contributor to *Odyssey* and a popular speaker, she's been featured on C-Span2 and RIF. Visit her animated moon at www.mariannedyson.com.

Robert Elmer is the author of more than thirty novels for kids, including the HyperLinkz and AstroKids series. He also writes stories for grown-ups, but he's too much of a kid himself to stop writing about fun things like space stations and the Internet. He and his wife, Ronda, have three college-age kids and a dog named Freckles; they live in the Pacific Northwest. Visit Robert's website at www.RobertElmerBooks.com.

Randy Ingermanson has a Ph.D. in theoretical physics from the University of California at Berkeley. He is the author of several novels about Mars and time travel and has won two Christy awards for his fiction. He lives in San Diego with his wife and three daughters.

Shane Johnson, a writer, graphic artist, and spaceflight historian, is author of the Christian adventure novels *The Last Guardian*, *ICE*, *Chayatocha*, and *A Form of Godliness*. He also served as producer/director for the video documentary *Apollo 13: Flight for Survival*, and was a design consultant for the award-winning HBO miniseries *From the Earth to the Moon*. Some of his earlier works include the Star Trek reference books *Mr. Scott's Guide to the Enterprise* and *The Worlds of the Federation*, and *The Star Wars*

Technical Journal. He lives in Texas with his wife, Kathy, and son, Daniel.

John B. Olson received his Ph.D. in biochemistry from the University of Wisconsin, Madison, in 1995 and did postdoctoral research in computational chemistry at the University of California, San Francisco. He is the author of the fast-paced thriller *Adrenaline* and is the coauthor of the award-winning novel *Oxygen* and its sequel, *The Fifth Man.*

Kathy Tyers lives in Montana and is the author of ten science fiction novels, including *Shivering World.* Learn more about the Elleh and their history in her Firebird trilogy—*Firebird, Fusion Fire,* and *Crown of Fire.*

Credits

Page 15: Mars photo courtesy of Space Telescope Science Institute. Background image © Michael Carroll.

Page 26: Images © Michael Carroll.

Page 48: Images © Michael Carroll.

Page 59: Images © Michael Carroll.

Page 72: Earth photo courtesy of NASA/JPL, the Galileo mission.

Page 113: Mars photo courtesy of Space Telescope Science Institute. Background image © Michael Carroll.

Page 128: Ganymede photo and background image courtesy of NASA/JPL, the Voyager project.

Page 142: Moon photo courtesy of NASA/Johnson Space Flight Center, the Apollo project. Background image © Michael Carroll.

Page 159: Earth photo courtesy of NASA/JPL, the Galileo mission.

Page 167: Images © Michael Carroll.

Page 218: Mars photo courtesy of Space Telescope Science Institute. Background image © Michael Carroll.

Page 235: Mars photo courtesy of Space Telescope Science Institute. Background image © Michael Carroll.